DOTTY'S SUITCASE

OTHER BOOKS BY CONSTANCE C. GREENE

A Girl Called Al
Leo the Lioness
The Good-Luck Bogie Hat
The Unmaking of Rabbit
Isabelle the Itch
The Ears of Louis
I Know You, Al
Beat the Turtle Drum
Getting Nowhere
I and Sproggy
Your Old Pal, Al

DOTTY'S SUITCASE

CONSTANCE C. GREENE

THE VIKING PRESS
NEW YORK

$2-80

First Edition
Copyright © Constance C. Greene, 1980
All rights reserved
First published in 1980 by The Viking Press
625 Madison Avenue, New York, N.Y. 10022
Published simultaneously in Canada by
Penguin Books Canada Limited
Printed in U.S.A.
1 2 3 4 5 84 83 82 81 80

Library of Congress Cataloging in Publication Data
Greene, Constance C.   Dotty's suitcase.
Summary: During the Depression 12-year-old Dotty's dream of traveling seems
remote until she finds money from a bank robbery and sets off with a companion in
a snowstorm to visit her best friend in a neighboring town.
[1. Depressions—1929—Fiction] I. Title.
PZ7.G8287Do   [Fic]   80–10949   ISBN 0–670–28050–x

For Audrey Benson
who cried with me in the movies
a long time ago

DOTTY'S SUITCASE

CHAPTER 1

"I DON'T WANT TO KNEEL," JUD SAID. "I WON'T IF I DON'T want to."

"You must," said Dotty Fickett. "I am the princess and you are my servant. You must kneel when I tell you to."

"You don't look like any princess to me," Jud said. "You can't make me if I don't want to. You just try and make me."

"Oh, come on, baby. Don't be a spoilsport."

"Don't call me baby," Jud said, scowling. "I'm eight years old and that's no baby and you know it."

"But I'm twelve," Dotty said in her most princess-like voice. "I'm older than you by far. I am the one who decides what is what."

"Who says? Why don't you pick on somebody your own

3

size?" Jud demanded, his eyes bright with spite. "I'm just a little fella."

Dotty whirled in a huge circle, causing her burlap cape, which she had made from old feed bags she'd found stored in the barn, to swirl about her in a very satisfactory manner. Then she reached out her long arm and got a grip on Jud's shoulder.

"One minute you say you're not a baby and the next you tell me you're just a little fella," she said. "Make up your mind." She tightened her fingers. "Your bones feel like a chicken's bones. If I wanted, I could crush you into a pulp. If I felt like it."

Jud stood still as a stone, nostrils flaring, breathing hard. She let go. "I have this to say and I will say no more. When I get my suitcase, I won't take you with me if you don't obey my commands."

"So?" Jud said. "So? When you getting it? You been talking about getting it so long I thought you already had it," he added, untruthfully and with malice. If Dotty had gotten her suitcase the whole world would've known.

"When I get my suitcase"—Dotty let her tongue move slowly, deliciously over the words—"I'm going on a long journey that I was planning on taking you on also. We will go first to Africa, I believe. We will take a small boat up the Nile."

"You got seasick that time we went fishing on the lake," Jud observed.

"There are many alligators on the Nile, my dear little friend," Dotty continued. She was pleased to see the look on

4

his face when she mentioned alligators. It was growing increasingly difficult to keep Jud in his place. He seemed to think that because he was now eight he was gaining on her. She had tried to explain that she would always be four years older, therefore four years wiser. He rejected this.

"I don't want to go to Africa," Jud said. "There's lions and tigers there and they bite."

"Who told you that?"

"My brother!" Jud shouted triumphantly.

"What does he know? Has he ever been there?" Dotty asked scornfully. "When we get there, we'll send him a postcard with pictures of mango trees and ostriches and crocodiles. And things you never dreamed of." Dotty's voice went slow and soft, like the hypnotist she'd heard last summer at the carnival. "There's gold and jewels of great price in Africa. And dancing girls with diamonds in their belly buttons."

Jud's jaw dropped. "Diamonds in their belly buttons?" he said in a hoarse voice. "How'd they get there?"

"They were born with them there," Dotty said in the same slow and dreamy voice. "Didn't you ever hear of babies born with diamonds in their belly buttons? It's God's way of saying the female is superior to the male. I myself was born in such a manner."

"You never," Jud said, narrowing his eyes. "If you got one, show it."

"I removed it in the dark of the moon and sold it for a king's ransom," Dotty said, closing her eyes and smiling at the memory.

"You're lying!" he hollered. She had pushed him too far. "You never had a diamond in your old belly button and you know it. Besides," he said slyly, "if you sold it for a king's ransom, why don't you go buy yourself that old suitcase and stop talking about it?"

Sometimes Jud surprised her. "You know nothing, wastrel," Dotty said in a singsong. "You know less than nothing, little turd. Here"—she threw aside her cloak—"come close and look sharp. There are still a few diamond chips left. If you look carefully, you may see them glittering in the light."

Jud crept close.

"See!" she cried. "See?"

"Looks like your old undershirt to me," he said sourly.

Dotty wriggled, pulling at her clothes. When she felt the cold air on her stomach, she cried, "See!" again.

Jud squinched up his face so he looked like an old man deep in thought. "I don't see anything," he said. "Not a blamed thing."

Dotty whipped her clothes into place. "You must need glasses," she said.

"Give me another peek!" Jud howled.

"Sacred scripture decrees that only one look is allowed to a mortal," Dotty intoned. "Perhaps another day when the moon is in eclipse."

"You're a cheat and a liar!" Jud shouted.

The sound of a bell rang out across the field. "Hark!" Dotty said. Jud stopped in mid-shout. "Hark," she said again.

The sound of the bell was very loud, very imperious. It called for instant obedience.

"It's your old Aunt Martha," Jud said. He took off up the hill.

"Liar!" he flung over his shoulder, on the run. "Cheat!" He disappeared into the bushes.

Alone, Dotty picked up a stick and brought it slowly down upon the shoulder of an imaginary figure kneeling before her.

"I deem thee Knight Jud in the name of Princess Dorothea of the royal family," she said in a dignified voice.

The wind sighed a secret message through the trees. An early owl hooted a reply.

Dotty drew in a long breath, lifted her face, and shook her fist at the sky.

"I shall live forever and ever!" she shouted. "I am invincible. I am indestructible. I am . . ." In vain she tried to think of something else she was and failed. The bell clamored again, telling her it was the last time and she had better come without delay.

Dotty broke into a gallop and headed for home.

CHAPTER 2

"I DECLARE, DOTTY," AUNT MARTHA SAID, SQUINTING fiercely at her, "I don't know what you do to yourself. I put lots of starch in that old dress last time I did it up, and look at it. It looks like an old dishrag."

Dotty looked down at herself. She thought it a very satisfactory dress, covered as it was with blue and white polka dots and possessing puff sleeves. Both her sisters had worn it before her. She loved that dress. The skirt flapped against her legs in a fine fashion, and she tied the half belt as tight as it would go without giving way at the seams.

"I can't let down that hem one more time," Aunt Martha said. "It's down as far as it'll go. And your socks." Aunt Martha's eyes roved the ceiling, and with her tongue she made clucking noises. "Never saw anything like your socks. From the back it looks like you don't have on any socks at all."

"I know," said Dotty, trying to pull her white socks up out of her brown oxfords and failing. "It's like there's something down there, quicksand maybe, sucking them down inside. I can't help it."

"And I swear I don't know what you do to your hair," Aunt Martha continued. "Washed it only two days ago and just look at you." She circled Dotty. "Looks like you been rubbing bear grease into your scalp."

"Bear grease is good for the hair," Dotty said. "And it also wards off evil spirits and keeps away flies."

"Oh, you! You and your tall tales." Aunt Martha grabbed Dotty and hugged her. "I just wish you'd find some nice little girls to play with, girls your own age," she said, releasing Dotty, "instead of holing up with a book all the time or bossing that little Jud boy around."

"Can I help it if Olive moved?" With a start of pure pleasure, Dotty felt her eyes fill and her lips tremble.

I am Katharine Hepburn. I am Jo in *Little Women*, and Beth is dying. Dotty squeezed her eyes shut, forcing the tears down her cheeks. *Little Women* was a movie she would remember for all her days. Except for *A Farewell to Arms*, starring Helen Hayes and Gary Cooper, *Little Women* was her favorite. She and Olive had gone to see it to celebrate Olive's birthday. Olive had made so much noise crying at the end that people had turned to stare. Dotty had skinned across the aisle to another seat so no one would know they were together. When they came out into the sunshine, Olive's eyelids were swollen almost shut, and Dotty had to lead her to the drugstore where they were to cap the day by having a black-and-white soda. It had been a memorable day.

And now Olive was gone, all the way to Boonville, seventy miles away. It might as well have been seven hundred miles. Olive's father had picked up and moved his family practically overnight when he heard of a possible job to be had in Boonville. In 1934 jobs were hard to come by. He'd been out of work for some time. Without a by-your-leave he had announced they were going, and they went.

"You've got to learn to make new friends," Aunt Martha said, her back to Dotty, wiping off the top of the stove. "Just because Olive's gone doesn't mean you can't make new ones. Take a leaf out of your sisters' book and be a mite more sociable." She turned and saw the tears coursing down Dotty's cheeks.

"Lands, child," she said, stricken, "I didn't mean to hurt your feelings."

"I was thinking about Katharine Hepburn as Jo in *Little Women*," Dotty explained. "It wasn't you. As for my sisters, I wouldn't be like them for all the tea in China." She blew her nose and wiped her face.

"No danger," Aunt Martha said wryly. "No danger whatsoever. You look pale. You take your tonic?"

"I am pale. I am always pale. I can't help it. I was born pale and I'll die pale."

"Most folks do."

"I have been reading *The Secret Garden*," Dotty said, to

10

change the subject. "Have you ever read it?"

"Don't believe so. Sounds nice. What's it about?"

"Well, this ugly little girl comes from India where her parents have been killed in a cholera plague," Dotty said, "and she goes to live with her eccentric uncle in a house on the moors in England. If I ever get my suitcase," Dotty went on, "that's where I'll go, first thing. To the moors in England. That's where my heart is, that's where I long to go. I think in one of my other lives I was a girl who lived in a cottage on the moors. What do you think you were in your other life, Aunt Martha?"

"Don't talk foolishness, Dotty," Aunt Martha said sharply. "I am what I am and have always been. This is the only life I've ever had, and when I die, I hope and pray I will go straight to the good Lord and that He'll be gentle with me."

"When I die," said Dotty, "the world dies with me."

"There's too much talk of dying," Aunt Martha said. "I don't hold with such things. I don't like you saying things like that."

"I didn't say it," Dotty said. "I think Emily Dickinson did."

"I don't know any Emily Dickinson."

"She was a poet. 'When I die, the world dies with me.' That's very profound. Think about it. 'When I die . . .'"

"That's enough," Aunt Martha announced firmly. "Time to scrape the carrots and get them in the stew. I'll leave everything ready so when the girls get home you can go ahead and have your supper. Your daddy will be late tonight, so you start without him."

Dotty went to work on the carrots. "Don't you want to hear any more about *The Secret Garden*?" she asked. "I have a great deal in common with Mary, the girl in the book. As I said, she's ugly."

"You're not ugly, child," Aunt Martha protested. "You're a nice-looking girl and bound to get better."

"I've got nowhere to go but up," Dotty said, but she was pleased, if not convinced, that her aunt was right and she would indeed get better looking in time.

"You have a very nice smile," Aunt Martha said, smoothing the hair off Dotty's forehead. "When you think to use it. And your hands and feet are just like your mother's. Long and thin. Don't know where she got those hands and feet. No one else in her family had anything like 'em. They were aristocratic-like. We used to tease her, say she got 'em from the king of the gypsies or someone like that."

Dotty flung herself at her aunt, almost knocking her off her feet. "King of the gypsies!" she cried. "I wouldn't be surprised if you're right. Why didn't you tell me before? My darling little mother," Dotty said, dancing around the kitchen and finally plopping down in a chair. "A gypsy queen!"

"Get on with your secret garden story," her aunt said. "You got my curiosity going."

"Well, this little girl's name was Mary," Dotty continued, "and she's very unpleasant, ordering everyone around on account of she's been living in India, as I said, and has always been used to a lot of servants."

Aunt Martha nodded. "There's them as knows how to

treat servants and them as don't. I've had experience with both kinds."

"Mary had an ayah, you see," Dotty explained. " 'Ayah' means 'nurse' in Hindu, and Mary's ayah obeyed her every command. Tied her shoes, brushed her teeth, dressed her, everything. The poor thing didn't know how to do one single thing for herself. And she bossed her old ayah around so she naturally thought she could boss everyone around, even these people in the house on the moors. But the people there wouldn't put up with her for a minute." Dotty scowled. "It was her uncle's house in Yorkshire, which is in England, you see, and in Yorkshire they weren't used to such terrible manners as Mary had. But it wasn't really her fault she had such bad manners."

"I don't hold with young folks telling their elders what they should do and not do." Aunt Martha shook her head disapprovingly. She exchanged her apron for her old gray coat. "That Mary child has to learn that's not right and proper. Someone will have to teach her some manners, and that's all there is to it." She laid her cheek on the air for Dotty to kiss.

"I best be getting home or Uncle Tom will think something's happened to me."

"I'll come with you!" Dotty cried. She looked at the clock. It was 5:25, almost time for her favorite program, *The Singing Lady*. She turned on the radio so that when she got home The Singing Lady's voice would be filling the room, almost as if she were there in person, warm, friendly, like a mother's voice might be.

13

"Don't fuss," Aunt Martha said. "I can manage alone."

"I want to fuss!" Dotty cried.

"Well, then, if you're coming, put on something warm. That cape wouldn't keep a flea from freezing," Aunt Martha ordered, already out the door.

"Anyway"—Dotty followed her, still wrapped in burlap—"this Mary had a very sallow complexion. She'd been sick a lot, you see. 'Sallow.' That's a word I must use more often."

"Don't imagine you'll have much call for it," Aunt Martha commented. "You left the door on the latch, did you? Won't be gone but a minute."

"Make haste," said Dotty, "for the night is coming."

"There's nothing to fear in the night if your conscience is clear," Aunt Martha said, putting one foot in front of the other as fast as she was able. "When I was a child, I was afraid of the shadows. But now that I'm old, I know there's nothing there. If you're coming, get a move on." She journeyed down the path so swiftly her skirts belled out, and she moved so rapidly, so smoothly it was as if she wore roller skates.

They traveled silently for a minute or two.

Dotty caught up. "As I was saying, Mary has this sallow complexion and no one likes her because not only is her complexion sallow but also, as I told you, she's very bossy."

"People shouldn't hold a person's looks against them," Aunt Martha said as she sped toward home. "A pretty face can hide a heap of sins."

"But you see, it wasn't just her face, it was her bad

14

disposition," Dotty said, her breath coming rapidly. Aunt Martha might be old but she was fast on her feet.

In the failing light Dotty could see her aunt nodding. "A bad disposition is the worst thing in the world," she agreed. "Almost."

Nothing moved but the wind and the birds and the creatures of the field. The light left the sky and Dotty Fickett shivered.

"I can see your house, Aunt Martha!" she cried. "I'm going back now. Good night, good night! Parting is such sweet sorrow!"

Aunt Martha lifted her hand in farewell and continued on her way. Dotty turned and raced toward home. Halfway there, she stopped, stamped her feet like an Arabian stallion, and whinnied to the empty sky. Her breath caught sharply in her throat and she whinnied again, half expecting an answering whinny. In an instant the wind died, and in the silence Dotty heard the sound of a door closing. The sound of a door closing in an empty house is a strange and lonely sound.

CHAPTER 3

THERE WAS NO ONE THERE. SHE WAS SURE OF IT. I AM not afraid. I am not afraid. Olive said if you repeated something many times, you began to believe it. I am not afraid.

Dotty leaned against the house, looking in, ready to run if someone looked out at her. I am an intruder, come to rob this place. As long as I remain on the outside, on the porch, I'll be all right. This I know for a fact.

Inside, the kitchen was the same, untouched, in order. The stew pot was stewing, sending out little puffs of delicious smells from under its lid. Aunt Martha's discarded apron hung in limp disarray on its hook. The kettle sat on the back of the stove, as complacent as a cat. The big old clock in the corner ticked away the silent minutes as it had always done. And on the wall, in its usual place, hung the picture that Dotty loved. It showed a lively, gay young woman squinting into the sun, holding up for the world's inspection a baby. That baby, as hairless as a baby bird not yet out of the nest, was Dotty. Her mother looked so proud. So proud. A short while after the picture had been taken, Dotty's mother had died, leaving her father with a sad heart ("I never saw a man so sad," Aunt Martha had told Dotty), three little daughters to clothe and feed, a rattly old car, and his hardware store, which provided them with a meager living. Luckily for them, Mr. Fickett's oldest sister, Martha, came to live nearby with her husband, Tom, and things looked up a bit. Martha had no children. She gathered the Fickett girls to her heart, cherishing and scolding them as if they'd been her own. They couldn't have managed without Aunt Martha.

A sneaky blast of wind crept around the corner of the porch and crawled inside Dotty's cape, making her shiver and stamp her feet. If only Olive were here, I would be brave. I know I would, Dotty told herself through chattering teeth.

Dotty hadn't believed Olive was really moving until she saw Mr. Doherty, with the help of Olive's three brothers, load the truck. First came all his carpenter's tools, then Mrs. Doherty's davenport. The davenport, covered in pale silk purchased years ago in Paris by Olive's grandmother, had stuffing hanging down in an abandoned and rather carefree manner, which spoke eloquently to Dotty of past glories.

"If she'd used some good sturdy material in a nice brown or gray," Aunt Martha had sniffed after she'd been to the Dohertys' for a cup of coffee, "it would've lasted a lifetime."

Then came the bed. Olive's four-poster bed, the most beautiful bed Dotty had ever seen and probably ever would see. Its slender posts were made of rosewood, rubbed smooth and fine, and it had once boasted a canopy of organdy and lace, Olive told Dotty in hushed tones.

The bed was the family treasure, although only Olive slept in it. It was a three-quarter bed, not wide enough for Mr. and Mrs. Doherty. Mrs. Doherty, though not known for her housekeeping, faithfully polished the bed once a week. All over. Not spit and polish. Everywhere. There was a hand-quilted blue-and-white coverlet, too, to add the final touch of elegance. Olive was not, of course, allowed to sit on her bed, and when Dotty went over after school, they always sat on the floor.

"You're not sitting on the bed, are you?" Mrs. Doherty invariably called out.

"No, Mama," Olive would answer.

The bed was Olive's inheritance from the same grandmother who had bought silk in Paris and whose picture was everywhere displayed in the Doherty house. The grandmother's face seemed to Dotty to be filled with disdain. She seemed to be saying, "You, out there, you are not as good as I. You are not as rich or as stylish or as anything as I am." Her eyes, set rather too close together to suit Dotty's taste, had a sly look, and her clothing held her flesh in a tight embrace, which may have been the reason for her somewhat strained smile and her prominent eyes that bulged out in a rather alarming fashion.

But what did it matter what Olive's grandmother looked like? She had handed down the beautiful bed to Olive, and that was what counted. The bed was a symbol of what had once been and would be again.

Olive's grandmother was also said to be widely traveled, which made her more interesting to Dotty than any other thing about her. She had been to any place on the globe anyone would care to mention. And some other places, besides. But Dotty had made a careful study of the many photographs of her displayed in all the rooms (there was even one of her in the kitchen!) and never once had she seen a suitcase. Never once. Not in one photograph.

When Dotty had asked about this lack, Olive had answered airily, "Oh, they have porters to load on the luggage. When you travel on an ocean liner, you don't carry on your own baggage." Olive had raised her eyebrows and trilled a laugh, unlike her usual laughter, which rocked the walls. "Mercy sakes, no!" she'd said, making Dotty feel like an ignorant peasant. Once in a while, even if they were the best, the truest of friends, Olive gave Dotty a pain. Not often, just once in a while.

An ocean liner. Dotty had been astounded. When she got her suitcase, she'd planned on taking a bus and maybe even a train or two, in addition to the small boat up the Nile she'd mentioned to Jud, but never, in her wildest dreams, had she thought of an ocean liner. New vistas, new possibilities of modes of travel were revealed to her.

Even now, standing on the porch, listening to the soft words, the music and songs coming from the radio, Dotty could see Mrs. Doherty, following close behind the four-poster, wringing her hands, imploring Mr. Doherty and her sons to be careful of the magnificent bed.

"Watch it, Pa!" she'd cried. "Careful of the sides. They're delicate. Boys, think of your grandmother! If anything happens to that bed, she'll come back to haunt us all." Thinking of the grandmother's face, Dotty shivered deliciously and thought, She will, too.

Finally Mr. Doherty had revved up the family truck, which had not been handed down by the grandmother but might as well have been. It too was an antique with delusions of grandeur.

Dotty could feel Olive's arms squeezing the breath out of her, could hear Olive's voice whispering fiercely in her ear, "You write me, hear? We can't be eternal friends if you don't write."

"Come along now. It's a long trip and we'd best be going." Mr. Doherty had shaken Dotty's hand, and Mrs. Doherty had pressed her dry cheek against Dotty's.

"Oh, how I'll miss you!" Olive had cried as the truck took off in a cloud of dust.

"Write to me!" Olive called repeatedly as her voice diminished, then was gone.

Now, standing on the porch, hands clasped for courage

and warmth, Dotty thought, If only I could go see Olive. If only. A finger of wind slipped inside a loose shingle on the side of the house and tapped an angry tattoo. Dotty jumped and almost cried out.

If they don't come by the time I count ten, I will go inside. I'll just go right in and listen to the radio. After *The Singing Lady* comes *Little Orphan Annie*. I like that program second best. I don't care who's there. I'll just go inside. Little Orphan Annie and Sandy will keep me company.

The wind resumed its fury, the shingle tapped out a secret message to someone waiting in the woods, and under her burlap cloak Dotty trembled.

CHAPTER
4

SHE HAD REACHED NINE, HAVING LINGERED LONG OVER both seven and eight, when she saw the lights of a car and heard Laura and Mary Beth sing out their thanks for the ride. Quick as a weasel, Dotty skittered into the kitchen, threw off her finery, and, snatching up a spoon, stood with it in her hand as if she'd been stirring all the long afternoon.

She fitted her face with a smile and kept it turned toward the door so they would see her there, smiling, the minute they came in.

"Home already!" she cried, incredulous, as they burst in, laughing and chattering as always.

"Oh, my poor feet!" Laura cried, taking off her shoes and

rubbing first one foot, then the other. "My poor babies!" she crooned.

"That's what you get for wearing such high heels," Dotty scolded. "You're too conceited about your feet."

Laura held one high-arched foot up for them to admire. Every time she managed to scrape together three ninety-five, she marched right off to A. S. Beck's over in Utica and bought another pair of ridiculously high-heeled shoes that killed her feet and, as Aunt Martha said, warped her toes.

"Wait till you see this!" Mary Beth said breathlessly, spreading the pages of a new magazine. "Dotty, put the kettle on like a good girl. Wait, Laura, until you see the gown and veil on the cover and inside, too. You'll die. Absolutely die. It's so gorgeous it almost makes me cry. It's the most beautiful gown I've ever seen." The two of them bent over, giving the pictures their full attention.

Dotty pulled her hair over her forehead, and from behind it she stared at her sisters. They are the two prettiest people I've ever laid eyes on, she thought. It's not fair. It's not at all fair that they look the way they do and I look the way I do.

"All you ever talk about is what you're going to wear when you get married," Dotty said in a cross voice. "It's very boring, if you ask me."

"Look at that! Just look at that crown made of seed pearls!" Laura cried. "Oh, wouldn't that be perfect! A crown of seed pearls! Can't you just see it?"

"With your hair," Mary Beth agreed, "but not for me. I think a lace veil held in place by a tiara would be nice. A lace veil," she said softly, "the color of cream. The exact same color of cream."

"When I get married, if I ever do, which I don't plan on doing," Dotty announced, "I will wear a long black dress with long sleeves and a gigantic train, and a tall black hat with a point on top like a witch's hat, and I will carry in my hands a poisonous black orchid."

"The water's boiling, Dotty darling," Mary Beth murmured. "Will you fetch a tea bag for me?"

Dotty plunked a tea bag into a cup and filled it with boiling water. "Besides, you're too young for that stuff."

"Too young?" Laura raised her eyebrows. "I'm seventeen. That's not too young to be thinking about things."

"And I'm old for my age," said Mary Beth, a year younger than Laura.

"If this old depression doesn't stop and folks start making money again," Dotty said, "nobody can get married to anybody because they can't afford to."

"What do you know?" Laura scoffed. "You heard what President Roosevelt said. 'The only thing we have to fear is fear itself.' If you're going to run around with your tail between your legs, scared of your own shadow, well, then, you're in trouble."

"Who says I'm scared?" Dotty asked in a loud voice. "I'm not scared of anything. Of the depression or anything else. What in the Sam Hill is that?" She poked a finger at a picture of a little kid dressed in a ridiculous white satin suit.

"That, Miss Smarty, is a ring bearer," Laura said. "He carries the ring around on a little cushion. Isn't he sweet!"

"Looks to me like he's carrying a pig that just died," Dotty said.

"See here!" Laura cried. "Look at this set of matched luggage!" She held up a picture of a smiling bride and groom cuddling a set of three suitcases in their arms as if they'd just had triplets. There was a small suitcase, a medium-size one, and a big one.

"Just like the three bears," said Dotty.

"Matched luggage is very elegant," Mary Beth said as if she knew. "You have your new initials put on it, and they give you a little key so you can lock the suitcase and nothing will be stolen. I think I would like a red suitcase."

D. F. F., Dotty thought. That's me. Probably no one else in the entire world has those initials. D. F. F.—Dorothea Frances Fickett. It's like fingerprints. No one else has the same set of fingerprints I do, either. The thought thrilled and interested her.

"I'm thinking of going to Hawaii," she announced. "To learn the hula-hula. I have always wanted to learn the hula-hula. I think I'll fill my suitcase with pineapples when I come back." Dotty continued to speak as if her sisters were enthralled with what she was saying, as if they were hanging on her every word. "I understand Hawaiian pineapples are the best in the world. I might also stop in San Francisco on my way home and swim in the Pacific Ocean."

Her remarks did not astound them, she saw.

She leaned forward to look at herself in the mirror, her face as expressionless as Greta Garbo's. She and Olive had seen Garbo in a movie, and both were impressed by her

25

beauty and the fact that no emotion whatsoever troubled the actress's classic features. They had practiced saying, "I vant to be alone," so many times that their voices grew hoarse and eventually they collapsed into giggles.

"I'm starving," said Laura. "When's Daddy coming home?"

"He's working late," Dotty said. She ladled out the stew. "Sit down. It's ready."

"Thank you, Lord, for this food and for all blessings," the girls said simultaneously. Their forks were on the way to their eager mouths before the words had a chance to settle on the air. They ate with hungry intensity.

Mary Beth was the first to finish. She always was. "I heard something today," she said, slowly scouring her clean plate with a piece of bread. "Something that I'm sure will interest you. Although"—she made eyes at Dotty—"I think she's too young."

Dotty looked unconcerned and kept her mouth shut.

"Oh, for Heaven's sake, Mary Beth," Laura said impatiently, "if she's too young, then you shouldn't have brought it up at all. What is it?"

"There's a woman," Mary Beth said slowly, getting up for another piece of bread, "a woman at the World's Fair in Chicago who dances." She stopped and again scoured her plate.

"Now you're being a pain. So what if there's a woman who dances at the World's Fair? So what? Finish what you have to say and stop leaving us hanging," Laura said.

"She dances stark naked," Mary Beth said. "Nothing

between her and the audience but fans. She dances behind these tremendous fans, and she's stark naked." Her eyes glittered and her cheeks were red.

Dotty kept her eyes on her plate and kept eating as if she heard things like this every day. Laura's eyes grew big and round as silver dollars.

"You don't mean it!" she said.

Pleased at the attention, Mary Beth smiled and nodded vigorously.

"Her name's Sally Rand and they say she's the hit of the entire Fair."

Dotty choked on a piece of potato. Absentmindedly Laura leaned over and pounded her on her back.

"Naked?" Laura repeated.

"As a jaybird." Mary Beth nodded.

"She must get awful cold," Dotty said.

"This girl I know said her uncle came for a visit, and he was telling her mother and father about this Sally Rand, and she eavesdropped." Mary Beth waved the bread at them. "And her mother said why couldn't the police stop such goings-on, and he said they tried and it was all legal and everything, and besides, she dances with these big fans in front of her and all so you can't see everything."

"Oh." Laura sounded disappointed. "So she's not really naked, after all."

"Listen, you try waving a couple of fans in front of you while you're in your birthday suit," Dotty said, "and see how much of your behind people can see."

"Don't be coarse, Dotty," Laura said primly.

27

"I wouldn't mind seeing this Sally Rand," Dotty said in a loud voice.

Both sisters turned and regarded her with shocked faces.

"What would Daddy think if he heard you?" Laura said.

"Wouldn't you like to see a naked woman dance?" Dotty asked. "Wouldn't you just?"

A silence, broken only by the sound of chewing, spread through the kitchen. Presently Laura, chin in hands, said softly, "I wouldn't mind."

"I'm not sure it'd be worth a trip all the way to Chicago," Mary Beth allowed. "If it was closer, I might go."

"Chicago might as well be Paris, France," Dotty said, "for all the chance we have of getting there. Might as well be Timbuktu, for that matter."

"Didn't you get to go to Utica last summer?" Laura demanded. "What more do you want?"

Dotty poked her fork through the last piece of carrot, spearing it, and lifted it to her mouth.

"Lots more," she said finally. "Lots more."

The sound of a car coming up the driveway silenced them. Dotty put her finger to her lips, telling them not to stir. She tiptoed to the door and turned the key in the lock.

Dotty imagined that the sound of stealthy feet on the front steps chilled her blood. She made herself walk slowly toward the telephone. She would call Aunt Martha. Aunt Martha would know what to do. But before she reached the hall where they kept their phone, a large, strong hand began pounding on the door. Then whoever it was took hold of the doorknob and rattled it.

"Let me in!" a voice cried. "Let me in at once!"

"It's Daddy!" Mary Beth cried. She ran to unlock the door. "Daddy darling, you look so tired. We thought you were going to be late. Come in and sit down and rest."

CHAPTER
5

THE THREE OF THEM CROWDED AROUND THEIR FATHER, helping him with his hat and coat, making little welcoming sounds. Laura and Mary Beth practiced on him, Dotty thought, standing back, observing. Even if he was only their father, he was a man and his presence acted upon them like strong drink. After they'd gotten him settled comfortably, they twittered about, cooing and trilling, ruffling their feathers, while Dotty ladled out the supper.

"We thought you were working late tonight, Daddy," she said, putting a steaming plate of stew in front of him. "Eat it while it's hot," she said in exact imitation of Aunt Martha.

"Yes, Daddy," the girls chorused, "we thought you were going to work late. We're so glad you're home."

Mr. Fickett picked up his fork and looked at it as if not sure what it was for. "I was going to go over my books," he said in his slow, measured speech. "Straighten out my accounts, try to get some of the outstanding bills cleared up. If I could afford it, I'd hire a lawyer to collect some of the money that's owed me. But I can't afford it so I keep sending out the bills."

"Your supper'll get cold," Dotty said.

He began to push the food around on his plate. "Then I turned on the radio and heard news of the robbery, so I locked up and came right home to make sure you were all right."

"What robbery?" Laura asked, exercising her dimples, smiling at her father almost the way she smiled at boys.

"You didn't hear?" He put down his fork. "A man robbed the bank today. Just as it was closing he came in and passed a note to the teller saying he was armed and wanted her to put all the money in her drawer in his suitcase. So she did as he said and pressed the alarm button at the same time. I'd like a cup of tea, please, Laura," and Mr. Fickett took off his steel-rimmed spectacles and rubbed the bridge of his nose, where the glasses had pressed two little red ridges in their effort to stay put.

Laura ran to make the tea. "Go on, Daddy," she said. "Tell us more."

"Well, something must've been wrong with the alarm because it didn't go off, so the man took the money and ran. The only other person in the bank at the time was old Mrs. Oliphant, and she's so deaf she didn't hear a thing. But she told the police she'd noticed the robber because he had such a mean face. 'Mean as a snake, he was,' she told them," Mr. Fickett said. "There was a car waiting outside the bank, an old black car with another man at the wheel, and they drove off and no one even got the license number. Thank you, Laura."

Dotty pushed the sugar bowl toward her father. "If I'd been there, I would've gotten it," she said. "I would've written it down in my head. How much money did they take?"

"I don't know, Dotty. Plenty, I guess. The bank has offered a reward for any information leading to the capture of the men."

"Oh, boy!" said Dotty. "How much?"

"I don't know. Don't believe they said. Turn on the radio and let's see if anything new has developed."

After a minute or two they heard the news. "The robbers made their getaway in what was believed to be either a Buick or a Studebaker at least ten years old," the announcer said in a cheerful voice. He seemed to be enjoying himself. "They are armed and dangerous, according to police." The announcer lowered his voice and became quite sober and important. "Anyone having any information leading to their capture please call the police immediately."

"How exciting!" Mary Beth said, her cheeks red, her eyes sparkling. "I never knew anything like this to happen around these parts. It's like living in a big city, Chicago or New York. That old Village Café will be crammed with folks talking about this tomorrow, you can bet your bottom dollar."

"This town will never be the same," Laura predicted. "This robbery will set this town on its ear for the next six months, if not longer, you mark my words."

"I bet those old robbers are lickety-splitting down the road right this minute at about a hundred miles an hour," Dotty said.

"A boy in my class is the son of the president of that bank," Laura said. "He's not stuck up or anything. But his father is the president of that bank. Imagine!"

"I bet they're counting that money and chuckling, laughing enough to split their sides," Dotty went on, "telling each other how smart they were. I bet they're planning on how they're going to spend it. If I had that much money," she said dreamily, "I know what I'd buy, first crack out of the barrel."

"*I'd* buy that wedding gown on the cover of the magazine," Laura said firmly.

"And *I'd* buy the lace veil the color of cream," said Mary Beth. "It'd be perfect with my coloring."

Dotty put her chin on her hands and said nothing. But later, much later, she remembered their conversation and smiled ruefully to herself.

"Well, Dorothea," Mr. Fickett said, after the older girls had gone off to wash their hair and to decide whether creamed chicken or filet of beef would be better wedding fare. "Come here, Dotty, and sit by me," he said. "If you had all that money, what would you buy with it?"

He passed his hand over her hair, just grazing her face. All

33

his daughters were dear to Dan Fickett, but somehow Dotty, his little one, reminded him so of his dear wife that every time he looked at her the tenderness rose in him, and the pain, and he longed to smooth her hair and pet her and tell her how much he loved her, but the words wouldn't come. He was not a man to express his feelings. After he'd turned seven, his own father had never again kissed him, and his mother had kissed him only when he got married and left home. And then only a peck on the cheek.

"Well, first," said Dotty, leaning against her father's side, making a warm spot there, tasting her words, "first, if I had that money, I would buy me a suitcase." She kept her head down as she said this, because somehow it seemed a shameful admission that with all those dollars in her hand she wanted such a small thing. "A suitcase with a brass lock and D. F. F. on it so everyone would know it was mine. No one else's, mine."

"Yes." Her father agreed. "I can see that would be a fine thing, to have a suitcase of one's own."

"Even if I don't go anywhere," Dotty said, raising her head to look at him, "it wouldn't matter. I'd have it waiting in case I ever did go someplace. I'd put it under my bed," she told her father, "and I'd take it out and look at it every night before I went to sleep, and keep it polished so I could see my face in it." She sighed and put her head against her father's cheek. "And if I can't have a suitcase," she whispered into his ear, "I'd like to be pretty."

Mr. Fickett closed his eyes and leaned his head back

against the chair. He cleared his throat, and after a minute he opened his eyes and looked at her, wordless. She put up her hand and stroked his cheek.

"But a suitcase is my first choice," she said.

CHAPTER 6

IN THE NIGHT MR. KIMBALL'S PIGS WOKE DOTTY WITH their yelling. She lay with her hands behind her head and thought about the sound of the door closing in the empty house. If Olive had been there, she would've barged in, hollering, "Who's there?", her red hair standing up as if charged with electricity, eyes flashing, fists clenched. Olive knew no fear. Instead, Olive lay tidily asleep in her four-poster bed over in Boonville, and neither the sound of pigs nor of doors closing disturbed her dreams.

You write me, you old Olive. You better. I know a stamp costs three cents. But you write me.

The pigs kept up their squealing. That meant a blizzard was on its way. Uncle Tom said that and he was usually right.

Uncle Tom was an authority on all of nature's weather signals. Pigs making a racket meant a blizzard, spider webs shining in the sunset meant a frost, frogs croaking in the rain meant warm, dry weather. Lots more.

Suppose the bank robber was hiding down cellar. Suppose he'd snuck in while Dotty was seeing Aunt Martha home. Most likely he was sitting down there, filling his stomach with last summer's preserves. Dotty got so mad at the thought that she turned back the covers and stuck out her foot. She'd fix him. It was cold out there. She dropped back to think things over and was asleep before her head hit the pillow.

Early next day, before the rest were awake, she crept to the cellar door and listened. There was no one there. She felt it in her bones. Just as well. She didn't feel much like doing battle. Funny how the morning took care of a lot of things. On her way to the bathroom she saw her father sitting on the edge of his bed, putting something inside his shoe. His shoulders were bent and tired looking, even this early in the day. Poor Daddy. There had never been a time in Dotty's memory when he hadn't been worried about money. The depression touched everyone, and although Mr. Roosevelt was President and lots of folks, except rich ones, had faith in him, he was only a man, not a miracle worker. Dotty never missed one of his fireside chats. The entire family huddled around the radio as if it were a huge, bright fire, and listened eagerly to the sound of his beautiful, persuasive voice, telling Americans that things were bound to get better. He sounded so vigorous and hopeful, so confident and sure of himself that just listening to him made her feel better. Mr. Fickett looked ten years younger while listening to Franklin Roosevelt tell how he was going to put the nation back on its feet. It was only after the radio had been turned off that his face fell into its familiar patterns.

Dotty sighed deeply, thinking about money and how too little of it wore people down and out. She couldn't imagine what it would be like to have enough money or—praise be!—too much. If there was such a thing.

Her father raised his head and looked at her, startled.

"I didn't know you were awake," he said.

"What're you doing?" She watched while he put on one shoe and tied it. Then he picked up the other one and she saw the hole in the sole. She put her finger through the hole, wiggling it and admiring the look of her fingernails since she'd given up biting them.

"Why don't you buy a new pair?" she asked.

He put out his hand and she gave him back his shoe. "Haven't had time," he said. "There," and he fitted the piece of newspaper he'd been folding over and over until it was nice and thick, into the hole, covering it completely so it might never have been. If she hadn't seen it.

"That ought to hold me for a while. When you're finished in the bathroom, Dotty," her father said, "wake the girls if they're not up, will you?" He smiled at her, and in the new light of morning he looked, for a minute, quite young, almost the way he did in the picture on his bureau taken with Dotty's mother on their wedding day.

There was nothing Dotty liked better than waking her sisters. Especially Mary Beth. More than anything else in the world, Mary Beth hated to wake up. She scrooched down under the covers, moaning, "Five more minutes. Only five. That's all I ask." Every day it was the same. When Mary Beth married her millionaire, she said she'd sleep as late as she liked, seven days a week. Laura, on the other hand, snapped open her eyes and sat up in bed, her hair as neat as if she'd slept sitting up. Laura was ready to spring from bed to attack the day.

"Rise and shine!" Dotty shouted.

Laura raised her head. "I wish you wouldn't say the same thing every morning," she said. "I can't bear it."

Dotty retreated, but not far. "Rise and shine!" she shouted again. Mary Beth started her moaning and Laura threw a heavy object, which just missed Dotty's ear. Probably a math book. That's what they usually threw. They never hit her, Dotty thought with satisfaction, but it was kind of tough on the book.

Jud's face was pushing against the glass in the door when Dotty got downstairs. Her father was drinking tea and eating a piece of toast and staring into space, not noticing Jud.

"Wait outside!" Dotty opened the door a crack and hissed. "We haven't even started breakfast yet." Jud came in anyway. He sat down opposite Mr. Fickett and stared at the toast, running his tongue over his lips.

"You hear about the bank robbery?" he finally said.

"What?" Mr. Fickett pulled his thoughts back from where they'd been. "Oh, yes. Yes. Terrible. I hope they catch them today."

The girls came clattering down. Their father put on his hat

and absentmindedly kissed his daughters, one, two, three. He almost kissed Jud, too, but Jud ducked just in time. This set Laura and Mary Beth to giggling so hard they bent over, clutching their stomachs. "Oh, oh, I'm going to be sick!" Laura cried.

"What's so funny?" Jud said, frowning. There was one piece of toast left on the plate, decorated with a smidgen of Aunt Martha's peach jam, which had taken many a prize at the state fair. He let his fingers wander toward the plate. No one was looking at him.

He almost had it. "No!" Dotty's hand came crashing down. "You're supposed to eat breakfast in your own house."

"I wasn't doing anything." Jud's face assumed a look of innocence. "My brother says he would've let those robbers have it if he'd been in that bank," Jud boasted, changing the subject. "He woulda crashed their heads against the wall, he said, and knocked 'em out."

"You want an apple or an orange?" Laura asked Dotty. It was Laura's week to make the lunches.

"Both."

"One or the other." She threw a spotted apple into Dotty's bag, along with a scalloped-edged cookie that looked as if somebody had gotten to it first. "Don't forget to stop off at Aunt Martha's. She probably has some shopping she wants you to do on your way home."

"Come on, let's go." Dotty dragged her hat down to her eyebrows and said good-bye to the girls.

Silently Dotty and Jud climbed the stone wall and made for Aunt Martha's.

Uncle Tom met them at the door, suspenders dangling, one side of his face smooth and clean, the other covered with shaving cream.

"Hear the pigs last night?" he asked. "Blizzard's coming. Nothing like '88, I'll wager, but a blizzard nevertheless. Why, in '88 the drifts were so high they swallowed up a four-story building over in Earlville. Whole herds of cattle froze standing up and they didn't even find 'em until the thaw. Now, *that* was a blizzard."

Last time she'd heard that tale, it'd been a three-story building over in Oriskany Falls, and Aunt Martha had said, "Tom!" the way she did when Uncle Tom was stretching the truth.

"On your way home, Dotty," Aunt Martha cut in, "will you pick me up a loaf of bread—make sure it's fresh—a pound of hamburger, and a quart of milk?" She handed Dotty thirty-five cents. "And make sure you count your change before you leave the store. You got to watch him. You don't count it while you're in the store, he'll say you must've dropped some on the road. I know him. You got to keep a sharp eye on him."

"Yes, Aunt Martha."

"And tell him last time the meat was too fatty. When I pay fifteen cents a pound for hamburger, I expect it to be lean."

Dotty pocketed the money and waited for further instructions. Apparently her aunt was finished telling her what to do and not do. Uncle Tom shaved the other side of his face, patted it dry, and saw them to the door. On the horizon the

41

clouds were building themselves into a high wall, and the wind was from the northwest.

"Bundle up good," he said. "And keep an eye out for the bank robbers. Radio this morning said they're still out there, preying on us innocent citizens. Got to watch for them. It's a big black car they're driving. Watch for it."

"Let's go," Jud muttered.

They hadn't gotten far, only to Kimball's orchard, where they'd picked all the apples they could eat or carry only a few months before, when Dotty clapped her hand to her head and said, "Sweet Jesus!"

"My ma says it's bad to swear," Jud said piously.

Dotty made a grab for him, but he leaped away in time.

"You know what?" she shouted. "He doesn't have money for his own shoes. That's why he's got to fit paper in the holes! Sweet Jesus!" she said again.

Jud turned around to see who she was talking to. There were just the two of them.

Dotty took off her mitten and with her newly long fingernails she pinched her own cheek so hard she almost cried out. She wanted to punish herself for having been so stupid about her father's shoe.

"Don't!" Jud protested, glad it was her cheek and not his. "It's bleeding."

"Is it? Good. I deserve to bleed." Dotty put the mitten back on, and they walked the rest of the way in silence.

CHAPTER 7

Dotty skidded into her seat minutes after the bell had rung, and Mrs. Murray hollered at her for being late. Bad enough but only the beginning.

"Hello," Janice Bailey said sweetly from the next desk.

"What are *you* doing here?" Dotty said. She felt her face go sour, like milk that's been left too long in the sun. Janice always had that effect on her.

Janice ran her tongue over her teeth and treated Dotty to one of her dazzling smiles. "My mother wrote a note to Mrs. Murray saying I had to sit nearer the blackboard on account of my eyes," she said. Janice's two front teeth got in each other's way and gave her a slight lisp, which she thought was

43

adorable. As a matter of fact, she thought everything about herself was adorable.

Dotty stretched her mouth into a wide Katharine Hepburn-type smile.

"Dear Janice," she said. "What would I do without you?" She fluttered her eyelashes at Janice, who looked startled, and turning to a blank page in her notebook, she began to write.

My father was dressed for church, in his striped suit and his new black hat. He carried his yellow doeskin gloves. His shoes were so shiny a person probably could have seen their face in them.

"You look very elegant, Papa," I said, putting my hands inside my squirrel muff.

My father bowed. "And you also, Daughter," he said, helping me on with my squirrel coat. "We will wait in the carriage for your mother. She will be down at any moment."

The butler opened the door for us and we went down the marble steps of our mansion.

"Ooooooh, you stop that!" Janice squealed joyously, bringing Dotty back to earth. The boy in back of Janice was stuffing his eraser down the back of her sweater. Boys were always stuffing things down her sweater, pulling her hair, stealing her lunch box. Janice planned on going to Hollywood when she got out of school. She planned on becoming a movie star.

"You think you're so cute," Dotty said under her breath. Aloud, she hissed, "You sound like Kimball's pigs."

"You quit that," Janice squealed again, "or I'll tell." She cut her eyes at Dotty and whispered, "Aren't boys awful?" and Dotty replied in a loud voice, "How would I know?"

"Come to order, class." Mrs. Murray handed out the papers from Monday's spelling test. "I'm happy to say we have two perfect papers and two almost perfect. To those of you who did so well, congratulations. To the others," and it seemed to Dotty that Mrs. Murray was looking straight at her, "I would suggest that they concentrate a little harder and study the words we've covered. I'll give another spelling test next week and will expect better results."

Dotty looked down as her paper was passed back to her. She shut one eye. It looked like a 76. It was. A big fat red 76. And spelling was her best subject. Mrs. Murray had drawn red circles around the misspelled words. *Imposible. Seperate.* And many more. Most of the words she'd gotten wrong she knew how to spell. She was careless, that's all.

I've got to pay more attention. I've got to concentrate. She rested her hand on her forehead and gazed down at her 76. I've got to earn some money. I feel old.

It seemed to Dotty that just beneath the edges of her memory were hiding many valuable lessons she'd learned but had, for the moment, forgotten. In her head was stored a wealth of knowledge, but she couldn't figure exactly how to get at it.

Beside her, Janice hummed a little tune. She shuffled her papers noisily and allowed one of the papers to slip from her grasp and slide across the floor to Dotty's desk, where it lay, face up.

45

She poked Dotty, pointing down at her paper. "Get it for me, will you?" she whispered. Wordlessly, Dotty clomped her shoe on it and pushed it back to Janice.

"Thanks," Janice breathed. "I wouldn't want to lose this. I'm going to take it home and set it up in the kitchen. My parents will be so proud."

She tossed back her hair, which was held in place by a pink ribbon which exactly matched her pink dress, and smiled her cross-toothed smile at Dotty.

What a waste.

To her rage and frustration, Dotty felt her eyes fill with tears. Only this time they weren't like Katharine Hepburn's in *Little Women*. They were like Dotty Fickett's in Real Life.

A different thing entirely.

CHAPTER
8

SOMEHOW, AGAINST ITS WILL, THE DAY SPUN ITSELF OUT. The bell rang at three out of habit, and Dotty put on her green wool jacket, the knitted hat of many colors she'd made for herself, and her galoshes and headed for home. Jud dragged behind her. It was Friday. The snow still held off.

"Don't forget the store," Jud reminded her. She had forgotten, but she didn't say, "Thanks."

"Hello there, missy," said Mr. Evans, the store owner and a church vestryman who never missed a Sunday and was not well liked in town. "What can I do for you?" His large red nose was crisscrossed by tiny lines that reminded Dotty of rivers marked on a map. His sleeves were rolled above his elbows, and his filthy, stained apron stretched itself taut against his middle. His hands were enormous, red and cracked, like his elbows. Dotty wondered if he was red all over, and didn't suppose she'd ever find out.

"They catch those robbers yet?" Mr. Evans leaned on his glass case, his voice jovial. "Imagine those boys are way over in the next county by now." He was not a jovial man, but he worked at it. Frequently he was heard hollering at his wife and kids at day's end. Being jovial when it's not your nature must be a strain, Dotty figured.

"What can I do for you?" he repeated in a sharper voice.

"I want a pound of hamburger, a quart of milk, and a loaf of bread. It's for my aunt," Dotty explained. "She said to tell you she wants the hamburger to be lean. She said last time you sold her some it was fatty."

"That aunt of yours is a caution." Mr. Evans threw back his head and laughed as if he had said something vastly amusing.

He put some meat on the scale and began adding to it, his hands the same color as the hamburger. While he was busy, Dotty sidled over to the magazine rack to see what was new. She kept close tabs on the movie magazines, careful not to miss anything. *Photoplay* was her favorite, with *Motion Picture* running a close second. They printed articles about what the stars ate, wore, showed pictures of the cars they drove and the rooms they slept in. Here was a picture of Carole Lombard's kitchen! Somehow the idea that Carole Lombard had a kitchen had never occurred to Dotty. This one didn't look as if it was ever used, but there was a picture of Carole, smiling, smiling, and whipping up what they said was an omelet. Imagine. And on to Joan Crawford's bedroom. Everything here seemed to be white. White rug, white bedspread, white sofas and chairs. Imagine keeping all that stuff clean. Still, Joan had maids and butlers to do the dirty work.

A thin woman wearing a hat that looked like a mushroom came in and asked Mr. Evans how much a stewing chicken cost. Mr. Evans took a chicken from his case and held it up by its feet. The chicken looked so much like a skinny little person that Dotty had to turn away in embarrassment.

The woman protested the price, but she said, "Cut it up and mind you don't leave out the giblets." Dotty went on to the *Saturday Evening Post*, which advertised on its cover an "Exclusive! New Pictures of Dionne Quintuplets!" Jud was leaning against the penny-candy case, breathing circles on the glass and drawing faces in the circles. It was a good thing Mr. Evans was busy cutting up the chicken.

Dotty opened the magazine to the right page. There were the Dionne quintuplets, five girl babies born all at the same time to a lady up in Canada. Entirely too much fuss was being made over those babies. You'd think they were one of the seven wonders of the world, the way folks were carrying on. There they were, ten beady eyes set in five fat faces, staring out at her. Dotty couldn't help wondering what Mrs. Dionne did if all five of those kids had a load in their pants at the same time. Mr. Dionne didn't look as if he'd be much help. He was a wispy little man whose face wore a look that

49

seemed to say, "Why me?" The Canadian Government had taken over the babies as wards of the state, it said in the magazine, which meant they'd pay all the bills: food, clothing, shoes, the works.

If there'd been five of me, Dotty thought, Daddy wouldn't have a thing to worry about. The idea of five Dotty Ficketts was astounding, even awe-inspiring. She wondered why she hadn't thought of it before.

"Here's your groceries," Mr. Evans said. "You want one of those?" he asked, poking a red thumb at the magazines.

"I want one but I don't have the money."

"Well, then, I guess that does it. That'll be twenty-seven cents." Dotty handed him the quarter and the dime and he gave her back seven cents. A nickel and two pennies. She counted it twice to be sure.

"I gave you thirty-five cents," she said. Mr. Evans wiped his hands down the front of his apron, leaving tracks, as if a dog had walked there.

"So. I gave you your change."

"You're short a penny. Twenty-seven from thirty-five leaves eight. You gave me seven. See?"

Mr. Evans' mouth fell open in amazement. "You're right. You're absolutely right. Some smart girl you are. Head of your class, I'll bet." He slapped another penny into her outstretched hand. "You tell your aunt that's the leanest hamburger she'll ever see. Tell her I killed the cow special for her." His laughter bounced off the ceiling.

Jud leaned against the penny-candy counter. "I'd sure like a licorice stick," he said.

"Two for a penny," Mr. Evans said, his red face redder than before.

"Don't got a penny," Jud said, studying his shoe.

"Me either. Let's go."

"Shut the door after you!" Mr. Evans shouted.

"You had a penny," Jud said accusingly as they went out into the cold.

"Move, slowpoke. It's not mine, it's Aunt Martha's." Dotty pulled up her collar and pulled down her hat so only a thin slice of her face showed.

"My hands are cold," Jud said.

"Put your mittens on."

He foraged in his pockets, his face gloomy.

"Got 'em?" Dotty watched as he put on the mittens. Then they climbed the incline leading to the highway, which went north. This route took them way out of their way. They took it only on Fridays, when the weekend and hours of free time loomed ahead of them. Dotty enjoyed watching the speeding cars going to Lord knew where, sometimes traveling as fast as forty, forty-five miles an hour. It was the only paved highway in these parts. The other roads were single-lane, bumpy dirt roads, which anyone who was in a hurry to get anywhere avoided like the plague.

As they reached the top, where they could get a good view of the traffic, a big black car zoomed by, going lickety-split. Up ahead, about fifty feet, loomed a sharp curve where there'd been several recent accidents.

"They better slow down or they're going to crash," Jud said. The car kept going, the driver hunched over the wheel.

51

As Jud and Dotty watched, an arm appeared at the window on the passenger side and threw something out. In a minute the car had disappeared.

The wind swooped down on them and tried unsuccessfully to carry them away. Dotty's knees knocked together and Jud's teeth chattered.

"Whwhwhatt was thththattt?" he asked.

"What was what?"

Jud's fists were like hard little rocks pounding on her. "You saw!" he shouted. "You saw somebody throw something out of that car and you know it!"

"You're seeing things," Dotty said in a bored voice. "Go on home. I'm going to take my time. You go on home before you freeze."

But even as she walked toward the spot where whatever it was they'd thrown had landed, she was certain she'd find something special, something she'd never seen before. Or would ever again.

CHAPTER 9

Whistling "the rose of tralee," dotty set off in the direction the black car had taken. Some days she could whistle pretty good. This wasn't one of them. The sound that came from between her pursed lips was a dismal sighing sound that might've been a lot of things, none of them "The Rose of Tralee."

When she turned to look behind her, Jud was standing where she'd left him, arms folded across his chest, eyes boring little holes in her head.

She had known it wouldn't work. "Oh, all right," she said. "Come on. But it's a waste of time."

"The robbers are still at large," Jud said, catching up. "The radio said they were. That means they're still out there"—his arm swept a large arc—"fixing to shoot some-body. The man said they had cruel eyes, mean like. Eyes like to cut you in two." He watched her face.

Dotty thumped her fists on her hips.

"You ever hear of Sally Rand?"

"Nope."

"She dances bare at the World's Fair." If that didn't take Jud's mind off the robbers, nothing would.

"Bare?" he whispered.

"That's the truth. Nothing between her and you except a big fan made of feathers. A gigantic fan made of feathers that'd float away if a big wind struck 'em."

She resumed her walking. He was behind her, quiet, thinking. Lord knows she'd given him something to think about.

They trudged along the shoulder of the road, careful to stay off the pavement. Presently the sound of a car, going even faster than the first one, reached them. They stood back until it passed. That car was going hell-bent for election, two men in front, two in back, all staring straight ahead grimly.

That car stirred up so much wind it made Dotty's galoshes flap against her legs.

"You see who that was?" Jud asked, his eyes huge. He made a pass at his mouth with his thumb. In times of stress Jud's thumb was a comfort to him.

Dotty glared at him. "Don't start that business now," she said. "I don't have time for a partner that sucks his thumb. No time at all."

Stunned by her use of the word "partner," Jud thrust his

hands into his pockets to avoid temptation and stomped behind her.

"It's got to be about here," Dotty muttered. She tramped in a small circle, head down, studying the ground, widening the circle as she went, beating down the dead gray grass, the mass of weeds.

"What're we looking for?" Jud asked, doing everything she did.

"If I knew that, it'd be easy, wouldn't it?"

"That was the sheriff's car," Jud said. "Him and his deputies were chasing somebody, I bet."

"Oh, they were probably just out for a ride," Dotty said airily.

"You know what? You got on your lying face. You know that was the sheriff good as me, and he wasn't out for any old ride. He was chasing somebody, and I bet you dollars to doughnuts he was after them robbers in that big black car." Jud's mouth clamped down. He was tired out, unaccustomed to making such a long speech.

"You keep your nose down and keep looking, otherwise go on home." Dotty made such a fierce face at him he cowered behind a pine tree for a minute.

Dotty retraced her steps, around and around, back and forth, and found nothing. She worked her way to the spot in the highway where the road curved. Whatever they'd tossed out they'd come back for. She was certain of that. Whatever it was, they didn't want anyone to find them carrying it.

"Suppose they come back?" Jud was so close to her she jumped. "Suppose they come back looking for what it was they threw out of the car? Suppose they find us here?" His voice faltered and died.

Dotty kept her head down. "They won't," she said firmly, not entirely believing it. "They won't. Keep on looking." If they came back and found me and Jud here, tramping around, searching for something, they'd probably kill us. They'd shoot us dead.

"We could look farther in," Jud suggested. "In from the road. Maybe that guy threw it way far in."

It was a thought. "I was just thinking that," Dotty said. They traveled back in and resumed their search. The light was fading fast.

"We better go home. I'm cold and I'm hungry, and besides," Jud said, "they might come back, and if they do, I don't want to be here."

"O.K." Dotty didn't want to be there, either, if they came back. Even as she spoke, her foot touched something that didn't feel like weeds or grass or an old beer bottle or anything like that. Whatever it was it was solid. Dotty knelt down to see better.

"It looks like a box," she said. The box lay partly hidden under a scraggly bush.

"Open it," Jud said softly, his breath tickling her cheek. "Open it quick."

"All it is is an old box," Dotty scoffed, her heart beating madly. "I wouldn't give you a nickel for it." She ran her hand lovingly over the surface.

Jud leaned down to look, his nose almost grazing their find. "Never saw no box with a handle on it," he observed.

"Looks like a suitcase to me. Is anything in it? Is it heavy? Lemme see if it's heavy." He tried to take the box away from her, and Dotty warned, "Hands off!"

"You're not the boss!" he cried, beginning to jiggle the way he did when he had to go to the bathroom.

"Pick it up. See what's inside," Jud said, jiggling madly.

"Go on behind that tree over there," Dotty said. "I won't look."

Jud scuttled behind the tree. Quick as a fox, Dotty worked the clasps on the box and the lid sprang open.

Even in the dim light she could see what the box held. She heard Jud coming back and slammed the lid shut, fastening it with shaking fingers.

"What do we want with an old box . . ." he began, then stopped.

"There's a car coming," he said.

Dotty stumbled to her feet, clutching the box. "Are you sure?"

"Listen yourself." He put a finger to his lips. "Can't you hear it? It's coming this way and it's coming fast."

Dotty strained her ears. He was right. There was a car coming. "Come on!" she whispered. Crouching low, she ran. Jud followed. They ran as fast as their legs would go, carrying them away from the highway, away from the approaching car, into the woods.

CHAPTER 10

"LISTEN HERE," JUD PANTED BEHIND HER, ABOUT TWEN-ty minutes later. "I got to rest. That's all there is to it. I got to rest." He made heaving noises, and she saw him put his head down between his knees. Nothing came up.

Dotty had a bad stitch in her side. It hurt something fierce. She leaned against a big old elm tree to get her breath. Then she stood taut, listening. In the distance behind her, there was no sound except the sighing of the wind.

"We forgot the hamburger," Dotty said at last. "Oh, my. Won't Aunt Martha be mad!"

Jud raised his head, and for a moment he looked very old and very wise.

"No, she won't," he said. "I got it." He tapped his bulging

pocket. "I got it right here, but I couldn't fit the milk. I had to leave the milk." He smiled, revealing the empty space in his gums that had recently held two teeth.

Dotty felt herself getting calmer. She held the suitcase close to the stitch in her side, as if it were a hot-water bottle and would help to ease the ache.

"Good for you," she said reluctantly.

Jud noticed the way she held the suitcase, the way she kept her eye on it, and he knew there was something worthwhile inside, no matter what it looked like.

"What you got there?" He pointed. "Let's have a look." He tapped his pocket again. "Don't forget. I remembered the hamburger. Just don't forget that."

"As if you'd let me," Dotty said sarcastically. "Wait'll we get home and I'll show you. Let's get home while there's still some light left. Come on."

They set out again. The tops of the trees stood out against the sky. There were no stars, no moon.

They walked for what seemed like miles, and although they stopped often to rest, the suitcase was getting heavy. She longed to put it down for another rest. Blood drummed in her ears, making a racket like the ocean pounding on the shore.

If only we'd come to a place I knew, Dotty thought, and there would be our house. Just as if we'd never left it. Smoke coming from the chimney, wash hanging on the line, Daddy's old car leaning on itself the way it does. If only.

Jud was beside her. "Up there. It's a light. I seen it."

"Where?"

59

"Right up ahead. It's gone now, but I seen it. I know I did."

"I have never been lost in my life," Dotty said indignantly.

"Me neither," Jud replied. "But there's always a first time."

"You make me sick." She turned on him. "You make me mighty sick."

His face assumed a slick, crafty look, full of guile. He was in charge, for a change. Wordlessly he patted his pocket that held the hamburger. Then he ran ahead.

"You know what?" he shouted. "It's the highway, that's what! We're back where we started."

He was right about the highway. Oh, Lordy, Lordy! Dotty came up behind him. "It's not the same place. There's no curve up ahead," she said in a scornful tone, glad to contribute something.

They saw headlights of an approaching car. It slowed and stopped alongside them.

"You kids need a lift?" the driver said, rolling down the window, leaning out. It was an old red pickup truck that, at the moment, looked good enough to be a movie star's limousine.

"Sure do." Dotty didn't recognize the boy, but was sure he must be from around here. Everybody was. "Come on, Jud," she called. He was right behind her, peeking out. "We got a ride."

"Toss your stuff in and let's get going," the boy said. "I got to be in Boonville tonight and I'm late."

Boonville? "You going to Boonville?" Dotty asked him, astonished.

"Sure am. That's if Bessie keeps going. Never can be sure. Some days she does what I tell her, some days not." He smiled, and in the light from the dashboard she saw and admired his golden hair curling around his head like tiny bed springs, and his teeth lined up in his mouth like kernels on an ear of white corn. He's pretty, she thought, almost as pretty as Laura or Mary Beth.

"My friend Olive lives in Boonville," Dotty said, boosting Jud up, then climbing in beside him. "Do you know her? Olive Doherty. Her father works in Boonville. That's why they moved there, so he could find work."

He shook his head. "Just toss your suitcase in back," he directed, putting his truck in gear.

"I'll just rest it here in my lap," Dotty said. Jud had his thumb in his mouth, making little clicking noises. When he sucked his thumb, he always hooked his index finger over his nose and peered over it, looking slightly moronic.

She decided he could keep it there for the time being. It kept him quiet, at least.

"It's not heavy," she said, cradling the suitcase to her chest. "It's light as anything."

He shrugged. "Up to you," he said, and they were off.

"How long will it take to get there?" Dotty asked.

"About an hour and a half—two, maybe. I'm not coming back your way, though. How'll you get back?"

He had nice eyes. He was very handsome, about seventeen

or eighteen. Too bad he wasn't going to drive them home. She closed her eyes and imagined herself pulling up in front of her house with this handsome stranger at the wheel. Of course, the girls would be peeking out the window as he helped her out and escorted her up the steps. She'd ask him in for a cup of coffee, and then, if Mary Beth and Laura behaved themselves, she'd introduce them to him.

They'd go crazy, she thought, smiling at the thought. Oh, well, I can't have everything, she told herself, not at all sure this was true.

"There's a bus that goes from Boonville to Earlville," she told him, as if she'd planned the trip carefully. "Twice a day, I think. Me and Jud'll take the bus."

"You got money?" the boy asked, his eyes on the road.

Beside her, she felt Jud's thumb stop its ticking.

"A little," she answered. "Enough for the bus. And if we don't have enough," she added, "my father'll give it to the bus driver when we get home. Besides, we won't need any money once we get to Olive's. They'll be so glad to see us. I can hardly wait."

"Seems like you two are a mite young to be out on the road at night," the driver said.

"Well, I'm thirteen." Dotty lied a little. It was only a white lie. She'd be thirteen next birthday. A white lie was all right to tell as long as it didn't hurt anybody.

"I've done some traveling." Once you'd told one white lie, the next one came easier. "Being the youngest in my family and all, I'm pretty grown-up for my age."

She could feel Jud's eyes on her, gazing stonily at her over the hump his finger made on his nose. He said nothing. And if he did, she'd give him her elbow in his ribs.

She shifted her body away from him, turning toward the driver so she couldn't see Jud watching her. He made her nervous. She never could be sure what he might come out with.

"I can call Mr. Evans up when we get to Olive's and tell him to let my father know where we are." She stretched her mouth into a smile and longed for dimples. "Mr. Evans owns the general store and he has a telephone. He doesn't mind taking messages."

Jud said, very low, "How would you know? You never give him none."

Expertly she gave Jud a tiny taste of the elbow. She felt him pull away from her.

"I'll tell him to tell my father we'll be home on the bus. It'll be perfectly all right. Daddy won't mind.

"My name's Dotty Fickett." Her voice rang in her ears. To her it sounded smooth and sophisticated, as if she did this sort of thing every day. "And this is my friend Jud. Well, actually"—she gave a small laugh—"he's more like my little brother than a friend. He lives nearby and his mother likes for me to look out for him."

In the darkness Jud made a little gagging sound. She increased the space between them and hoped fervently the noise he made was one of disgust and not carsickness.

"Pleased to meet you," the boy said. "My name's Gary."

With a thrill of recognition, Dotty thought, Of course! That's who he looks like. Gary Cooper. Oh, my! Clasping her suitcase firmly, she settled back in her seat as the truck hurtled toward Boonville at thirty-five miles an hour through the black night.

Her heart was working overtime, flipping around inside her like a fish out of water. She took a long, deep breath. Everything up to now had been pretend. This was an adventure. For real. She and Jud were on their way to Boonville with a suitcase. And what a suitcase!

It was almost too good to be true.

CHAPTER
11

DREAMS CAN BE DISTURBING. LULLED BY THE WARMTH and motion of the truck, Dotty dozed. Aunt Martha appeared before her, wringing her hands, calling Dotty's name. Then Olive was there. She and Olive were in a strange house, dressed up in old sheets, as if it were Halloween and they were ghosts. Only Olive had painted a wide red mouth over her own mouth. "I'm Joan Crawford," she said. So Dotty drew a mouth on herself, but the color got all over her face and even her teeth were pink with lipstick. Olive began to cry, and her mascaraed eyelashes ran in black rivulets down her cheeks. She was a mess. When Dotty asked her why she was crying, she shook her head soundlessly and cried harder. It was terrible.

Dotty woke with a start. The truck had pulled up to a gas station in the middle of nowhere. In the single pale light that shone from a dirty window Dotty could see the first faint beginnings of the storm. The snowflakes worked their way down from the sky in a deceptively lazy, uncaring fashion, as if they meant no harm, had no particular destination in mind.

A man slouched toward them, rubbing his eyes, probably angry at having his nap disturbed. Jud lay heavily against her arm, and the suitcase seemed to have gained in width and weight.

Gary's hand rested lightly on the suitcase's handle.

"I was going to put it back where it'd be safe," he said softly, smiling at her.

Dotty sat up straight, tightening her grip. "It's O.K. How much longer till we get there?"

He opened the door and jumped down. "Forty-five minutes, hour. Depends. Be right back. She'll take five gallons," she heard him tell the man as he made for the rear of the station.

I should go to the bathroom too, Dotty thought. But the idea of leaving the warm truck and going out into the night didn't appeal to her. She'd have to take the suitcase with her. She'd leave it with Jud, but he was asleep and she didn't want to wake him.

She took off her hat. Her head itched. She'd never worn the hat for such a long time before.

She stretched it out over the suitcase. Even in the dim

light its colors were bright and clear. She wished she had a comb. It would be nicer if her hair were combed. There was no sense in rummaging through Jud's pockets. He didn't know what a comb looked like. Every time his hair got long enough to get hold of, his mother chopped it off with her dull scissors. Most times Jud's head looked as if the chickens had been scratching in it. After she'd knit her own hat of various bits and pieces of wool Aunt Martha had given her, she'd started on one for Jud. As a surprise. Then the next time she'd gotten mad at him, she'd told him she wasn't going to knit him a hat like hers after all. All he'd said was "Thank God for small favors," a favorite expression of his mother's, and her feelings had been hurt. She hadn't let him see that her feelings were hurt. Now wild horses couldn't make her knit him a hat.

Gary came back. "We got a ways to go," he said. "Maybe you'd better go inside." He jerked his thumb in the direction he'd taken. "This is the last gas station until we get to Boonville."

"I'm all right," she said. "I'm just anxious to get there."

"How about him?" He pointed to Jud. "You don't think you better take him inside?" He hopped up into his truck.

"I'll watch the suitcase for you," he said.

"It's all right," she said again. "Why don't we get going?"

"Have it your way."

And try as she might, Dotty couldn't go back to sleep. She wanted to, very much, so she could pick up her dream and find out why Olive had been crying. She kept her eyes closed

67

and willed herself to sleep. It didn't work. She thought about the money she was holding. How much was there? Enough for new shoes for her father?

"My Uncle Tom said we're in for a blizzard." Dotty opened her eyes and sat up straight. "Mr. Kimball's pigs were hollering, and Uncle Tom says that always means a blizzard's coming."

"That right?" He sounded bored.

Dotty thought, Why am I so boring? I bet I bore a lot of people. The more interesting I try to be, the more I bore people. Why don't I shut up and act inscrutable? I *am* inscrutable. Ever since Dotty had learned that word, she'd been looking for an opportunity to use it in a conversation. So far no occasion had arisen.

She wished she were older and could flirt with Gary the way her sisters would have. Or Janice. She would have liked him to look at her with admiration in his eyes, the way she'd seen boys look at Mary Beth and Laura. Even if you didn't think you'd recognize admiration in a boy's eyes, it was amazing the way you did once you'd seen it. Absolutely amazing. She must remember to tell this to Olive.

She felt her mouth shiver. She wanted to make him look at her and tell her she was pretty.

I've never been anywhere, she almost said aloud. And now here I am, going to Boonville in a truck with a stranger. Alone. Jud stirred in his sleep. Well, almost alone. Jud was the chaperon. The thought made her smile.

"Understand you people had a bank robbery over your

way," Gary said. Dotty's fingers tightened on the suitcase handle.

"Sure did," she said gaily. "Radio said the robbers were still at large yesterday. Said they were driving a big black car and that they were armed and dangerous and one of 'em had mean, squinty eyes. A lady saw 'em and that's what she said."

If anybody ever had to describe me on the radio, Dotty thought, what would they say? I am not the kind of person people remember. I have a forgettable face.

Dorothea Frances Fickett, alias Dotty Fickett, aged twelve and a quarter. Brown eyes, brown hair, and sallow complexion. Long hands and feet. Mole on left shoulder. Ugly.

But possessing a kind heart. Not always. Sometimes. I hope I have a kind heart. A pretty face isn't everything. As Aunt Martha says, a pretty face can hide a heap of sins. Think of Janice.

The truck racketed through the night. Dotty's head fell against Jud and he cried out in his sleep. He looked as if someone had removed all his bones, so relaxed and limp he might've been a large doll. Little drops of spittle ran down his chin, and she thought he was looking at her through the slits his eyes made.

She had never been out this late. Outside, there was nothing but blackness. Soon, she hoped, the lights of Boonville would shine in the distance. She stole a glance at Gary. And discovered he was stealing a glance at her. They stared at one another, as unblinking as a couple of babies.

"How old are you?" she asked, not having planned to.

"Sixteen," he told her. His bony white ankles shone in the darkness. He didn't seem to have on any socks.

"Your feet must be cold," she said.

"Not so's you'd notice." He gestured toward the suitcase. "That's pretty big for such a little girl. You must have all your duds in there. You planning to stay in Boonville awhile?"

"Oh, no. Only just the night. Olive's not expecting me, you see." Dotty felt her face grow animated, like an actress doing a scene. "Olive and I are best friends," she went on. He seemed to be listening, giving her his complete attention. It was an exhilarating sensation, to be given the complete attention of such a good-looking boy.

"Olive's father moved to Boonville to find work. But we write to each other all the time." Dotty's lips and eyes and hands moved in unison. She felt as if she were sparkling. Next to her, Jud stirred.

The snow was falling fast now, coating the roadway, making it slick.

"We're in for a big one," Gary said. His foot pressed down on the accelerator and the truck gained speed.

"Don't you think you ought to slow down?" Dotty asked. Up ahead she could see a car approaching. It seemed to be swimming at them through the snow. The wind picked up handfuls of snow and flung it at them as if they were having a snow fight. It was beautiful and exciting and scary. Gary leaned over the wheel, his face in the headlights of the oncoming car bright with the thrill of battle.

"Move over!" he shouted. The driver of the other car didn't seem to hear. As Gary grunted and wrestled to stay in control, the car swerved into their path, forcing the truck over to the right and into the woods at the side of the highway. A deep ditch separated the woods from the road. With a great shudder, the truck settled into the ditch as if it would never leave. And the car that had swerved into their path went merrily away from them, scattering snow in its wake into the black night, intent on arriving at its destination on time.

CHAPTER 12

DOTTY RESTED HER HEAD AGAINST THE SUITCASE AS IF IT were a feather pillow. And the suitcase, one of its sides caved in, rested itself against the truck's dashboard. Through the gap in the cardboard Dotty saw the brilliant green-and-white new money, arranged neatly in stacks, each bound by a strip of brown paper. The sight was blinding. She tried to push the broken sides of the suitcase together and failed.

Gary lay back in his seat, his eyes closed, a tiny trickle of blood running from his nose, which was small and pointy and might once have appealed to her. Funny she hadn't noticed his nose before. It looked to her sharp enough to poke a hole through a piece of paper. His chest moved up and down, so he wasn't dead. His cheekbones lay so close to the skin they looked as if they might break through at any moment.

The headlights of the truck shone as if nothing had happened. They cut a lazy path through the falling snow, which coated the windshield and enveloped the truck in a thick, heavy curtain.

Beside her, Jud jiggled. Oh, Lordy. Only Jud would have to go to the bathroom at a time like this.

"Can't you hold it?" she whispered.

He rolled his eyes at her and motioned toward Gary. When Dotty turned, Gary's eyes were wide open. He was looking at the money and smiling.

"Well, I declare!" he said in a high voice. He put out his hand and slid it inside the suitcase, where it stayed as if caught in a trap. He touched the money gently.

"I never," he said softly. "I figured you for a little something," he said to Dotty, "but never nothing like this. I guess this is my lucky day, eh?" He stretched his face into a ghastly smile, and she wondered how she could have ever thought he looked like Gary Cooper. The adventure was turning sour.

"I found it," she said, against her will. Jud jabbed at her. "We did," she said. "Jud and me. Somebody threw it out of a car and we picked it up."

"How come nothing like that never happened to me?" Gary asked. "Never found so much as a nickel on the sidewalk even. Never had two bills to rub together. Never. Been working since I was younger'n you too. Hey," he said softly, "my dad'll go crazy when he sees folding money.

73

Plumb crazy. Been wanting to help him out. Now I can," he said, grinning at her, becoming lively. "Guess I'll have to charge you for a couple tickets to Boonville. One way. Wouldn't want to cheat you none." He smiled, and she turned away.

"Travel's not cheap," he went on. "One ticket for you"—he thrust out his thumb but didn't touch her—"and one for the little punk."

There was a stillness inside the truck. Only the wind and the snow moved outside. Dotty swallowed and the noise was deafening. Jud huddled up next to her, and they waited for Gary to make the next move.

"Your nose is bleeding," she said at last. "Aunt Martha says you should put ice on the back of your neck to stop a nosebleed."

Gary wiped his nose along his sleeve. "We sure could use your Aunt Martha along about now, now couldn't we?" He reached over and took a couple of bundles of money from the gap in the suitcase. "Gasoline's high, costs twelve, thirteen cents a gallon, and this old buggy's a regular gas eater. And now she'll need repairs. A new fender, maybe, maybe even a couple new tires. Or maybe"—he ruffled the tightly bound bills with his finger so they made a slight breeze—"maybe I might better turn her in on a new model. A shiny, brand-new model. Whatdya think about that?" He winked at them.

"Jud has to go to the bathroom," Dotty said in a high, hoarse voice.

"Well, now. That's too bad." He shook his head. "Told

you you shoulda used them facilities at the gas station. Trouble with young folks these days is they don't listen. Never do what their betters tell 'em." He leaned past Dotty and cuffed Jud on the ear.

Dotty felt as if she were strangling. "You keep your hands to yourself," she said, the words jamming together in her throat. "I'll take him."

"No, you don't. You stay right here where it's cozy and warm, and make sure no burglars get in. I'll see the little punk does his business. It's gonna be cold in that bathroom, ain't it, little punk?" Gary opened the door and put one leg out into the storm.

"You stay here," he directed her, and to Jud he snapped, "Move!"

The door handle was slick under Dotty's fingers. She pushed down. It was now or never. She was afraid, afraid of Gary, afraid of the storm. The storm, she decided, was the lesser of the evils confronting them. They could hide inside it. It was their escape hatch. In the dark of the truck she clutched the suitcase and prayed.

Gary pushed open the door on his side. The wind grabbed it and tried to yank it out of his hand. "Make it snappy," he barked.

Dotty eased open her door. She said to Jud in a low voice, "When I jump, you jump. Then run like the devil." The door swung open, letting in the snow, which had been waiting for them.

"Jump!" she whispered. In the headlights they saw Gary coming around to their side.

She jumped with Jud so close behind she felt his foot hit the back of her legs. This is how it feels to bail out of an airplane, she thought. The snow folded itself around them like the cold fingers of a cold hand.

As they ran, it seemed to her, then and after, that Gary's voice surrounded them. He was hiding behind a tree, and when they drew near, he would spring out at them, throw them to the ground, take their money, and then stomp them to death. And leave them to the mercy of the blizzard. She was sure his pointy nose possessed extraordinary powers, that even through the wildness of the wind and the snow he could get their scent.

But he didn't spring at them. Once or twice she was certain she heard him. "Dotty! Jud!" he called. "Come on back! Let's go to Boonville." The wind sang in the trees. "Boonville!" it sang. "Go to Boonville!"

They trudged on, Dotty lugging the suitcase, holding it together with her frozen hands. Snow coated their clothing, their eyelashes, their eyebrows.

"You didn't go to the bathroom," Dotty said, as she remembered.

"I don't have to any more."

She pointed to a tree. "Go," she said. He went.

"What'll we do now?" he asked when he came back.

"We're not going back there, I can tell you that." She jerked her head in the direction of the truck. "He'd skin us alive."

"We're not?" The wind caught his words and tore them out of his mouth. "What're we going to do then?"

"First we get rid of this." She thrust her hand into the gaping suitcase, pulled out rolls of bills, and stuffed them inside her jacket. She did the same to Jud. His jacket was so filled with money he looked fat. "Here, put the rest in our pockets." Miraculously she transferred the money from the suitcase to their persons without the wind getting any of it.

"You said nobody threw nothing out of that car," Jud said, suddenly furious. His face stood out, crimson in the whiteness. "I figured us for pals. Pals share."

"I wasn't going to keep it. You know I was going to split it with you. Besides, Jud"—she put her face up against his—"there might be about a thousand dollars in there," she said in a whisper.

Even over the sound of the wind she could hear him catch his breath. A thousand dollars. Or a million. Or a trillion. They were all one and the same. Money to buy new shoes for Daddy, or a new car. Or both. Things for Aunt Martha and Uncle Tom. A tiara and a lace veil the color of cream for the girls. A suitcase with her initials on it for herself.

And with all that money surely she'd become pretty. All rich ladies were pretty. In the movies, anyway. There was no reason to think that riches didn't bring beauty. Except for Olive's grandmother. After a moment's thought Dotty decided to give her the benefit of the doubt. She undoubtedly had been beautiful when she was young. Or, at any rate, not so ugly.

It was odd. Now that they were out of the truck and into it, the storm seemed less ferocious than it had. They began to walk. Dotty tugged the belt of her jacket as tight as it would go to keep the money inside. Then she did the same to Jud. She pulled on his belt until he hollered, "You're cutting me in two!" They plodded on. It's still Friday, Dotty thought. Probably the longest Friday I'll ever go through. And it wasn't over yet.

"I think we should've stayed," Jud mumbled. "Where it was warm. With him."

"He would never have let us go," Dotty said. "When it got light he would've killed us and thrown our bodies out and driven off and they'd never have found us. Animals would have eaten our bodies, and nobody would ever have known what happened to us."

"You think so?" Jud's eyes were huge. "I bet they're worried about us. I bet they're pacing the floor, up and down, up and down, wondering what happened."

"The minute we get to Boonville I'll call Mr. Evans and he'll take the message to them." Dotty pushed the thought of Daddy and the girls and her aunt and uncle out of her head. By now they would be frantic. She could hear Aunt Martha saying in her wry voice, "That's Dotty. Act first, think later." All the more reason for them to leave the truck and try to find a ride to Boonville. Or, second best, a ride home.

Jud turned in a circle, batting his eyelashes to get rid of the snow that collected on them. "Do you think he's following us?" he whispered. "Do you think he's going to get us?"

"Not if we keep moving."

"I sort of thought you liked him," Jud said slyly. "At first."

"He was mean clean through. Could've told you that."

Dotty stared at the ground. "Watch your step. Stay close to me."

"Didn't you like him at first?" Jud wasn't one to let up.

"Are you crazy?" Her voice was loud and tough. "I sure wish we'd see a car. Keep moving."

"Suppose nobody comes? There's not many cars out on a night like this. What do we do then? We should've stayed with him. They'd find us sooner or later."

"He might have killed us. And he sure would've stolen all the money."

"Well," Jud said philosophically, "if we was dead, we wouldn't miss the money much."

"Oh, shut up," she said. "Keep moving and keep quiet."

In the dim light she could see Jud smiling at her. "I'm going back," he said.

"No," said Dotty. "Wait for me."

He was gone in an instant. In the flick of an eye. Swallowed up by the storm.

I am alone in the universe. I am Eliza, crossing the ice. I am at the South Pole assisting Admiral Byrd. I am on the verge of discovering a lost continent. I could scream at the top of my lungs and no one would hear me.

"Come back!" she shouted. No answer. Again she shouted. The wind had been sucked back into the sky. Silence and snow gathered her up in their frigid arms. She turned to look back, to see if Jud was fooling and getting ready to pounce out at her. She could see nothing. Only swirling snow. The wind, howling again, sounded like a wolf. Like a pack of wolves.

79

The thin, swift wings of fear began to beat in her head. We haven't gone very far from the truck. We just set out. Only five minutes ago we were inside the warm truck and Gary was taking money out of the suitcase where it had cracked wide open when the truck went into the ditch. Gary was only sixteen. As old as Mary Beth. Sixteen was too young to be evil. He was too good-looking to be evil. The expression on his face when he saw the money flicked in front of her like a scene from a movie. He'd called Jud "punk" and hit him.

She spun around, thinking she'd heard someone call her name. She couldn't be certain. Snow whirled in her eyes, up her nose, slapped at her face. She opened her mouth to call Jud again, and it too was filled with snow.

I'm not lost. If I go in this direction, I'll see the truck in the ditch with Gary and Jud in it and I'll just get back in it until the storm's over. He won't hurt us. I must stay calm. I know exactly where I am. I'm almost to Boonville. To see Olive. In a minute I'll see the truck.

But when she turned, what lay behind also lay ahead. There was no horizon, there were no familiar landmarks. There was nothing but blackness and biting wind.

I won't call Jud again. He's snug as a bug right this minute. I'll be there too, in a second. Please, God, don't let me be lost again. Not twice in one day. I can't stand it.

Dotty stood still, trying to get her bearings. The snow made sad little whistling sounds as it settled in for the night. I must keep going. I mustn't sit down and rest. No matter how tired I get, I mustn't stop walking. If I do, I might freeze to death. I have read that freezing to death is like going to sleep.

80

When I die, the world dies with me.

Snow caked her galoshes, making each foot weigh a ton, each step an effort. This is what it must be like to be old, Dotty thought.

She heard someone crying. Very faint but clear. Crying like a lost babe in the woods. She listened again and heard nothing. Her imagination was playing tricks. Then she heard it again. It sounded like a small child.

"Dotty," the voice wailed. "I'm here, Dotty."

It was Jud. You little weasel, she thought joyfully as she struggled through the snow in the direction of the cry. I thought you were lost. I thought I was lost. Now that I've found you, I'm not lost any more. All is well. You little weasel. Maybe next time you'll listen and not go on without me.

If there was a next time.

When she reached him, he was lying in a snowdrift, crying. She had never heard him cry, and there'd been plenty of times when he'd had reason to. Jud was lots of things but never a crybaby.

"I'm tired!" he wailed. "I can't get up. I'm too tired. I want to take a little nap. Not a big one, just a little one. Then I'll come with you."

"No, you don't," she snapped. She wanted him to give her an argument so she could get mad at him. It would give her something to do. Instead, he put out an arm, and she grabbed it and tugged him to a standing position. He stood there, weaving back and forth. "See? I told you. That wasn't hard, was it?"

She felt very powerful, very wise, much older than he. She'd gotten him into this mess and she'd get him out. Together they'd get out.

"Let's head for the truck," she said.

Jud's eyes shone in the dim light. She saw him nod. "You start and I'll follow," he said.

Dotty drew a deep breath. He thought she knew the way. Let him. It couldn't be that hard to retrace their steps and go back as they had come.

We are at the North Pole and a Saint Bernard will find us and lead us home. No, I think Saint Bernards only find people in the mountains in Switzerland. Never mind. This is a Saint Bernard dog at the North Pole, which happens to be in New York State near Boonville.

"I'm cold," Jud said. He put his mittened hand trustingly in hers, a thing he'd never done before. If he'd cried or whined or been a brat, she could've scorned him, made fun of him. But he was depending on her, and that made her afraid.

"What's the matter?" he said when she didn't move.

She waited a minute, thinking a miracle might occur, something or someone would show them the way. The minute passed. "I think we're lost again," she finally said. The wind attacked from all sides. "I'm pretty sure we are," Dotty Fickett said.

"We could pray," Jud said at last.

"I've already tried that."

"Maybe God couldn't hear you over the wind. It makes a terrible racket. Try a little louder. I'll help."

"O.K.," Dotty agreed. "Kneel down."

"No siree!" Jud shouted, jumping back. "You're not getting me to kneel down in all this snow. No siree! I'm not doing it."

So they stood upright and said, "Our Father, Who art in Heaven." She continued but Jud only mumbled the words. It was clear that "Our Father, Who art in Heaven" was the only part Jud knew. Dotty went to the end and stopped.

They waited, silent in the storm, holding their breath so, in case God decided to send them an answer, they'd hear it. None came.

"I knew it wouldn't work," Jud said glumly. "And I don't care what you say," he added, cantankerous again, a good sign. "I'm sitting down for a rest. I'm tired. I don't even know what I'm doing here. I'm dead on my feet."

"And I suppose I'm not!" she screeched at him. "You're the only one who's cold and tired? You can't sit down! I won't let you! You'll freeze to death and I'll get the blame. If anything happens to you I'll get the blame because you're eight and I'm twelve and I'm supposed to know better. They always blame the older kid when something happens. You know that. And I'll tell you this." She shook her finger at him in the dark. "I'm not going to be responsible for you. You get up from there right this minute or I'll tell your mother."

"Tell her what?" Jud asked. She yanked him to his feet. He was small but solid. But I am responsible, she thought. If it wasn't for me, he wouldn't be here. Why did he have to follow me?

"Please, Jud, please," she begged him. She could just

83

make out the pale blur of his face as he turned to her and said, "Dotty, do you think they'll find us?"

Keeping the fear out of her voice with a huge effort, she said, "We'll be fine. Should see a car soon. We'll be just fine. Long as we keep moving."

"But do you think they'll find us?" he persisted.

Who was "they"? "Probably," she answered. Then a great surge of tiredness overcame her, and she said, "I don't know. I just don't know."

There was nothing more to say. They were running out of hope. They plodded on, stopping at intervals to peer into the bitter darkness. There were no cars out on this night; there were no lights. There must be an end to this, Dotty told herself. We can't just keep going. We should've stayed in the truck. There must be an end.

Suddenly Jud started forward. "I see a light!" he shouted.

"Where?" she asked dully, not believing him.

"There. Through there. A little light it is. A light, I tell you!"

She saw nothing.

"It's a mirage," Dotty said. "Like when people get lost in the desert and they're dying of thirst and up ahead they see a water hole and when they get there there's nothing. It's only a mirage."

"My foot," said Jud. "I see it, and I smell smoke. Somebody's got a fire going." He began to run, and in an instant he was swallowed up by the storm.

For the first time Dotty knew complete panic. Now she was alone. Only the sound of the wind and the feel of the

84

snowflakes hitting her face kept her company. She kept going because she had no choice.

Head down, she plodded onward, hand in hand with despair.

"Dotty!" a voice cried. "Over here, Dotty!" It was Jud, hollering fit to burst his lungs. "Over here!" The sound trailed off, borne away by the wind.

She lifted her head. Through her snow-covered eyelashes she could see a small and pale and glorious light shining, telling her to come, to follow it home.

"Daddy!" Dotty sobbed. She started to run. It was amazing how strong her legs had become when, minutes before, they had been limp and exhausted, almost without life.

"Daddy!" she cried again as she ran toward the light and the warmth it promised, and safety.

CHAPTER 13

THE LITTLE HOUSE WAS EMPTY. THEY HAD COME TO THE end of a long and perilous journey, and there was no one to bid them welcome. Even as they mashed their noses against the window and peered in, they knew the room would be empty. Ashes glowed in the fireplace, and a large pot sat in solitary splendor on the stove, promising untold delicacies.

They banged on the door. "Is there anyone there?" Dotty cried. There was no answer.

"Is there anyone home?" they cried again and again.

There was no answer.

"I don't care," Dotty said at last. "I'm going in."

"I'm scared," Jud said. "Maybe they're hiding."

"Suit yourself. I'm going in." Dotty pressed down on the latch and the door swung open. She stepped inside, Jud right behind her.

"Hello! Hello! Hello!"

There was no answer.

"They can't be far," Dotty decided. "With the fire still going and all. Let's knock on that door." She pointed to the end of the room. "Maybe they're asleep." She knocked on the door. Silence. She turned the knob. The door creaked open with a long sigh, as if it hadn't been open in years. Jud jumped.

"Suppose he's under the covers?" He looked at the large, untidy bed that was the only piece of furniture in the room. "Suppose he jumps out and gets us?"

"Anyone in here?" Dotty shouted. He, whoever he was under there, might be deaf.

The covers stayed quiet. They closed the door gently and went back to the stove. Dotty laid her hand on the pot's side. It was warm.

"I'm having some," she said.

"What is it? I might not like it," Jud said.

"Who cares?" Dotty found some dishes and spoons on the table. "You want some or not? This is your last chance."

Reluctantly Jud said, "Give me some."

"Please."

"Please."

She ladled it out and they ate. It was delicious. Vegetables and potatoes and some kind of meat. Jud leaned his elbows on the table and made disgusting noises as he ate. Dotty frowned at him and said nothing. She didn't have the strength.

"What'll we do now?" Jud asked, his eyes glazed with fatigue.

"Sleep," she said. They lay down in front of the fire, still wrapped in the soggy warmth of their outdoor clothing.

Jud hooked his index finger over his nose and slid his thumb into his mouth. Dotty started to say her prayers. Halfway through, her mind emptied itself of everything, and they both slept.

CHAPTER 14

WHEN DOTTY AWAKENED, MORNING WAS CREEPING timidly through the window, as if it were afraid it might not be entirely welcome. The room was filled with the smell of sleep. The fire had gone out. It was very cold.

A tall man stood watching her. In each hand he held a bundle of money. Their money. Hers and Jud's. "That's mine," Dotty said sharply, sitting up. She saw her jacket and hat lying, neatly folded, on the back of a chair. She knew she hadn't put them there, had, in fact, worn them when she lay down to sleep.

"So it is," the man replied, frowning at the money as if it had done something wrong.

"It belongs to Jud and me," Dotty said belligerently. It was *his* house, after all, she told herself.

"Didn't say it didn't. I wondered what made you kids so lumpy." The man's clothes were brown and wrinkled, like his face. "You must admit it's something of a shock when a man comes into his house and finds two lumpy kids stretched out, dead to the world. Couldn't figure out what made you and the boy so lumpy." His face wasn't unfriendly. "So I took off your jackets and things so you'd be more comfortable, and look what I found." He put the money on the table and threw two logs on the fire to get it going again.

"I must say I was glad to discover what made you such an odd shape. Would you like some breakfast?"

"Yes, please," said Dotty.

"If you want a wash, there's a bathroom through there." He gestured with his thumb. "And there might even be soap and a towel."

He poked the stove and put on a pot of water. Dotty went into the bathroom and washed. She was stiff and still tired, but she was alive. The thought was strangely exhilarating. They had survived.

She sat at the small, rickety table and watched the man stir oatmeal into the boiling water. Wait'll Jud found out what was for breakfast!

The silence stretched out. The man asked no explanation of her presence here and seemed to accept it as a matter of course.

"We were lost in the woods," Dotty said. "And we saw your light so we came in. But first we knocked on the door over and over. The house was empty and we'd come a long way in the storm and we were tired."

The man nodded. "It wasn't a fit night out for man or beast," he said.

"Where were you?" she asked.

"Out for a walk. I always walk at night, no matter what the weather. It was a magnificent storm, wasn't it?" He turned toward her. "The excesses of nature have always been a splendid mystery."

He put down a bowl of oatmeal in front of her and offered a jug of milk and some brown sugar. "White sugar's bad for your teeth," he cautioned as if he were her father or Aunt Martha.

"You want to let him sleep?" He pointed to Jud.

"Oh, yes, for a little while. He's only eight, you see. I'm twelve so it wasn't so hard on me." Her voice rang righteously in her ears.

He nodded in agreement. "That's true. The older one gets, the better one is able to stand up to adversity. Until one gets very old." He sat down and they ate their oatmeal.

Dotty's spoon scraped the bottom of the bowl. "It was good," she said. "The best oatmeal I ever had."

"I'm a pretty fair cook," the man said. "And getting better all the time. Where are you bound for with all that money? California? I understand they have more salubrious winters in California than we do here." His face was long and homely, his eyes kind. "I'm not sure it's a good idea for two kids to be on the road with all that cash. Never can tell what might happen."

91

"We found it," Dotty said. She told him about seeing something thrown out of the big black car and how they went to investigate, about finding the suitcase in the weeds.

"So we picked it up and ran because we thought the man who'd thrown it was coming back," Dotty went on. "We got lost. Then a boy picked us up and he was going to Boonville and I have a friend in Boonville named Olive Doherty and so we decided to ride with him and he got in an accident and it turned out he found out about the money and he wasn't so nice so we ran away and we got lost again and it started to snow and"—she shrugged—"here we are."

Jud sat up, rubbing his eyes. "Who's that?" he asked.

"Sorry," the man said. "My name is Rufus P. Clarke." He put out his hand, and he and Dotty shook hands.

"I'm Dotty Fickett. And this is Jud. He's not my brother—he's just a neighbor. We go to the same school. He's eight—or did I tell you that?"

"I believe you mentioned the fact. It's a pleasure to have you both. I don't have many visitors, living out here. Practically none, in fact." Idly he ruffled the bundles of money.

"What's he doing with our money?" Jud asked rudely.

Dotty shot him a fierce glance, telling him to mind his manners. "He took off our jackets so we'd sleep better and he found it."

Mr. Clarke went to the stove and ladled out a bowl of oatmeal for Jud. He brought it back to the table.

"Don't worry about your money, Jud," he said. "Sit down and eat while it's hot. I've given up on money."

Jud stood with his hands behind his back, frowning at the bowl of oatmeal.

"Eat," Dotty commanded.

"How come you gave up on money?" Jud asked. "I never heard of anybody doing that before. What is it?" he asked, sitting down.

"It's delicious," Dotty said. "Eat."

"Well, it's the root of all evil, sometimes," Mr. Clarke said. "Money can cause a lot of trouble."

Jud leaned on his elbow and stirred the oatmeal thoughtfully. Then he put his head to one side, as if he were listening to strange voices. "I never had any so I wouldn't know," he said at last.

"Me either," said Dotty.

"Well," Mr. Clarke said slowly, reluctantly, "I used to have a lot. A big house and cars and everything that went with them. A wife and two beautiful children. Then I lost everything in the stock market and suddenly I found myself without the house and the other things."

"But you still have your wife and your children," Dotty said quickly.

"No," he said. "My wife left me. She took the children with her." Jud's spoon stopped in midair. His mouth dropped open. Dotty could see the unchewed oatmeal inside. She turned away, unable to bear the sight of it or the look on Mr. Clarke's face.

He continued with his story as if hearing it for the first time. "It wasn't just the money. To be fair, I don't think she minded losing it as much as I did. I was too stern, too demanding. Not loving enough." He shot them a fierce glance. "I spent all my time making the money and none of it enjoying what I'd made. I blamed her for lots of things. I never blamed myself. That's the trouble. There's no one I can blame for my lack of caring, showing them I cared. No one at all. I put money ahead of everything."

Jud's spoon ricocheted wildly inside his empty bowl and made the only noise in the room. Dotty didn't know where to look. She had never heard, never imagined such talk. Except on the radio. Or in the movies.

"So," Mr. Clarke said at last, "I've taken to the woods. I rather like it. Solitude has many virtues. Makes you look yourself in the eye, think about things you thought you'd forgotten." He sat down at the table and folded his hands.

"If you can stand solitude," he went on, "you can stand yourself, and that's something a lot of people never find out: if they can stand themselves."

He smiled at them for the first time.

"If I had to choose between having a lot of money and none at all, I'd choose none. Makes life a lot simpler, having none at all."

"Still," Dotty said, absently frowning at Jud, "still, it's better if you have a choice."

"A good point," Mr. Clarke agreed. He got up and went to the window. "Storm's about over," he said.

They looked out and watched a few snowflakes swirl aimlessly in the air.

"You kids put on your stuff. I expect it's about dry by now, and we'll have a path cleared to the barn in no time," Mr.

94

Clarke said. Sure enough, their jackets and hats were warm from the fire, their mittens stiff and dry, stretched out on the hearth. And Mr. Clarke had even stuffed their boots with paper to help them dry too.

"You thought of everything," Dotty said. "You took good care of us. Thank you."

"You're welcome. I'll have you in Boonville before you can skin a cat," he said.

"You will? How?"

"Hitch up Sarah and she'll have us there in short order." Mr. Clarke put on a vast brown overcoat and a hat with ear flaps which he pulled well down over his weathered face. "We're only about five miles from Boonville right now. You tell me where your friend lives and you'll be knocking on her door before lunchtime."

"Who is Sarah?"

"My horse. Don't know what I'd do without her. Dress warm now, and I'll be back for you in a few minutes. And don't forget this." His finger tapped the bundles of money lying on the table. "When you get back home, you'll have to find whom it belongs to and get it back to them."

"We think it belongs to the bank," Dotty said. "They had a robbery Thursday. We think the robbers were the ones who threw the money out of the car, on account of they didn't want the police to catch them with it."

Jud made a terrible dark face at her.

"I don't think that, she does. I think it's finders keepers, that's what I think," he said.

Mr. Clarke paused with his hand on the latch. "Here you

have a moral dilemma," he said thoughtfully. "You have a choice, after all, Dotty and Jud."

"I do?" they both said.

He took a shovel from the corner. "Sure. You can either keep the money and tell yourselves finders keepers, or you can return it to its rightful owner. In this case, the bank."

"They already got plenty of money," Jud said. "And we don't."

"It isn't theirs," Mr. Clarke said. "It belongs to the depositors—people like you. And me."

He opened the door. Snow was packed in a tight white fence up against it, barring his way.

"That's why I keep a shovel inside. The choice between right and wrong. Always a tough decision to make." He began to shovel. "Just let me get this out of the way and then shut the door behind me."

When he'd cleared away the snow fence, Dotty shut the door and thought about what he'd said.

Jud tugged on his boots. "You and your big mouth," he sneered. "You got a big mouth, Dotty Fickett, and that's the truth."

CHAPTER
15

THE SNOW AND WIND HAD RETREATED, LEAVING MASSES of heavy clouds sitting on the horizon, taking a breather. Each tree branch stood stark and still against the gray sky like a beautiful piece of sculpture.

If only I could paint, Dotty thought, I would paint this now, this minute, because when summer comes I will have forgotten how it was, how it looked, how it really was.

She watched as Mr. Clarke hitched Sarah to the sleigh. He looked different now, with his thick warm hat pulled well down over his forehead. Under it, his face looked abandoned. His long chin settled under his coat collar as he stroked Sarah's neck and told her to be a good girl, that they would soon be on their way.

"There's a nice girl," he told her. "Be patient. It's only a little while now and we're off to Boonville, Sarah, old girl. It's an adventure for us, isn't it?"

And Sarah sighed and whiffled through her nose at him and stamped her feet urgently, anxious to begin her journey. Sarah's nose was wide and pink and soft as a length of velvet, Dotty thought. Timidly she patted Sarah on her nose, then she hopped about on one foot, then the other, to keep warm.

Imagine going to Boonville to see Olive! And in a sleigh! She could picture Olive's face when they drove up. Olive would shout and holler and scream with joy! Dotty hugged herself in anticipation.

Mr. Clarke went into his cabin to get a warm lap robe for the trip. Jud scuttled into the barn just to give it the once-over. "I wish we could stay here for a while," he'd confided to Dotty. "I like it here."

Dotty walked toward the forest that surrounded the house. She imagined herself alone out here, in the midst of nowhere. Completely alone. It was God's will that she and Jud had found this place. If they hadn't stumbled on it, they might still be wandering.

Or they might be dead. Tears sprang to Dotty's eyes at the thought of herself and Jud frozen solid under a snowdrift. Daddy and the girls and Aunt Martha and Uncle Tom would carry her body back home and bury it under the apple tree after the ground thawed. It would most likely be May and the apple blossoms would be out, spreading their fragrance thickly over everything. Then people would go back to the

Ficketts' house, where the ladies would have a handsome spread set out in the kitchen, and everyone would remember Dotty fondly and tell tales of how kind and gentle she'd been, how she'd made everybody laugh. They'd talk in tender tones of how well loved she'd been. Dotty got herself so worked up, thinking of the day in May when she would be laid to rest, that she was filled with very fleeting regret that she and Jud had gotten out of the storm.

Mr. Clarke called from the cabin door for her to come in for a minute. He held up a small black case. "I found this," he said. "It'll be just right for you to carry the money in. It'll be safe inside this." Briskly he began to pack the bundles of money Dotty and Jud had stuffed inside their jackets.

Dotty took off her mitten and ran her hand over the surface of the case. It felt soft and smooth and, bending down, she sniffed. "It's leather, isn't it?" she asked Mr. Clarke.

He looked surprised. "Of course," he said. As if suitcases were ever made of anything but.

"Oh, no," Dotty said softly, keeping her hand on the handle. "I can't take this. It belongs to you."

There were brass fittings and a tiny lock, and imprinted on the case were the letters R.P.C.

"It's beautiful," she whispered.

"It's of no matter," he said gruffly. "It's something I once used and no longer have any use for. I don't even know why I brought it with me except, I suppose, I needed it for my socks or something. I want you to have it." He put in the last of the money and snapped shut the fastenings.

"Have you got a key for it?" Dotty asked.

"I did have. Once." Mr. Clarke patted his pockets as if he thought the key might jump out and into his hand. "It's lost now, I guess."

"Now you got it." Jud's eyes and voice snapped at her in unison. "That's what you been after all this time. A suitcase. Now you got it and you can go to Africa."

His lips curved over his teeth at her, and she thought he was smiling, but she couldn't be sure.

"I'm glad you'll get some use from it," Mr. Clarke said.

"I'll bring it back." Dotty planted herself firmly in Mr. Clarke's way so he'd be sure to hear what she had to say. "I promise I'll bring it back. It's too nice to give away. It's got your initials on it."

"I don't want it. It's yours," he said. "It will give me pleasure to know you're enjoying it. Now you two hop in and we're off."

Mr. Clarke tucked in the blanket and climbed into the sleigh. "Aren't you going to lock your house?" Dotty asked.

"Giddap, Sarah," he said. "What for? There's nothing worth taking and maybe someone else will take shelter there while I'm gone."

Sarah snapped her head up and down, pawed the ground and turned to look at them, checking to see they were all there.

"How long will it take us?" Dotty asked.

"About an hour, I should think. I've only been to

100

Boonville once, soon after I came here, and I don't really remember. But we should move right along. Giddap, Sarah," he said again, and they began their journey to Boonville and Olive. With money in a suitcase.

CHAPTER 16

QUESTIONS DOTTY WANTED TO ASK MR. CLARKE chased around in her head.

How old are your children? What do they look like? Do they write to you? Do they love you?

But she didn't dare put her tongue to any of them.

Sarah's breath made milky inroads on the air; her hooves clip-clopped rhythmically as she carried them through the woods. On either side the branches of trees, bowed down by the weight of snow artfully arranged on them, brushed the sides of the sleigh, setting wild flurries in motion. Underneath the scratchy blanket, which smelled of horse and barn and other pungent things, Dotty warmed her hands on Mr. Clarke's suitcase as if it had been a hot-water bottle.

Presently they came out of the woods. Ahead of them stretched what seemed to be miles of flat, unbroken whiteness. The snow, like a giant eraser, had wiped out everything. Fences, meadows, hedges, orchards, ponds, roads—all were gone. Even the animals must be snowed into their burrows as there were no animal tracks as far as the eye could see.

The sleigh soared across the snow like a sloop with its sails full of wind. Or a Russian sledge zooming across Siberia, a pack of wolves in pursuit. She was the Princess Dorothea, daughter of the Czar, fleeing her father's enemies, who were gaining on them. Or, better yet, Mr. Clarke was the king's equerry and, still the Princess Dorothea, she was on her way to a ball. Jud was her page.

As if he guessed her thoughts, Jud shot her a sour glance. His eyes slipped around in his head as if they'd been oiled.

"I want to go home," he said, laying the words down as if they were cards and he were playing Crazy Eights. And losing.

"What day is it, anyway?" Under the big peak of his hat, Jud's narrow little face peered out, his sharp chin and freckles dazzling in the light. "It feels like next year, we been gone so long."

She had to stop and think. "Why, it's only Saturday!" Dotty exclaimed, amazed that this was so.

Jud rolled his oily eyes around and made a snout out of his nose. "Seems like we been gone for years."

"You didn't have to come. Nobody asked you. It's not my fault we got in this mess."

103

"Whose is it then?" Jud asked innocently. "Whose is it?"

"Stop complaining," Dotty said, as if he hadn't spoken. "This is an adventure. We haven't even missed a day of school, for Pete's sake. Just stop complaining."

He snuffled loudly and she wasn't sure whether he was fixing to cry or was laughing at her. She turned sideways so she couldn't see him looking at her.

"Some people will always be a stick-in-the-mud," Dotty said. "They are born that way. They can't help themselves. They are just plain born to be a stick-in-the-mud."

They rode on in silence broken only by the sound of Sarah's hooves and the sudden noise of snow falling from the branch of a tree. After a time Mr. Clarke said, "Seems I've taken a wrong turn somewhere along the line. This doesn't look familiar to me at all. I think I'll stop up here and ask directions." He reined in Sarah as they approached a farmhouse curled under the brim of a small hill, a farmhouse with peeling paint and a porch that clung to the front of the house for dear life, fearful it might drop off at any moment. A battered mailbox bearing the name A. Lazlo stood at the end of the drive, and a sign swung from a large old maple tree, proclaiming: "APPLES. PICK UR OWN. CORTLANDS, MACS, ROME BEAUTYS." Dotty and Jud stayed in the sleigh as Mr. Clarke went up the front steps. A crowd of small faces looked out at them, pale and watery behind the cracked windowpanes.

A woman with a thin, irritable face came to the door. "Yes?" she said in a sharp tone.

Mr. Clarke took off his hat, and she moved back, as if she

thought he was going to hit her. "I wonder if you could tell me which road goes to Boonville," he said courteously. "I seem to have lost my way."

The woman smiled tentatively, as if her face were stiff and she'd forgotten how to smile from lack of practice. "Why," she said, "you ain't but a spit away. At the foot of the driveway, you turn left and then . . ."

"He turns right is better, Ma," a large boy corrected her, coming out from behind his mother's skirts, suddenly brave. "You turn left, you come to the old mill, you got to go around the pond. Takes twice the time. You turn right, you be better off. Takes you straight up to the highway, and it ain't but a short distance then." The boy stepped back behind the woman's skirts as if he'd said his lines in a play and were going behind the curtain, his part over. There was a sound of scuffling.

"Think they know everything, don't they?" The woman took a swipe at her coarse gray hair, pushing it behind her ears. Then she took another swipe at the surging bodies behind her, apparently engaged in mortal combat.

"Young 'uns don't mind their manners the way they used to. When I was a girl"—she smiled coquettishly at Mr. Clarke—"young 'uns had some respect for their elders."

Mr. Clarke thanked her as if she'd given him the keys to the city. "You've been very kind," he said. The children giggled. Dotty stared angrily at them, sure they were making fun of Mr. Clarke because he was so polite. Jud had crawled so far under the blanket only the top of his hat showed.

Mr. Clarke took up the reins, chirping to Sarah, telling

her to giddap once again. Halfway down the driveway, Dotty looked back. The woman stood at the open door, looking after them, her hand to her hair. And at the windows the crowd of pale, watery faces pressed against the windows, misting them, watching the visitors leave.

"You warm enough?" Mr. Clarke asked after he'd turned right as the boy had directed him. His cheeks were rosy from the cold, and his face looked less desolate than it had.

"We're fine," Dotty told him. Beside her, Jud snuffled loudly. "Just fine."

She hugged herself and smiled in anticipation, thinking of how Olive would look, how astonished she'd be when she saw the sleigh in front of her house and who was in it. Why, Olive would shout and laugh and carry on something terrible when she saw Dotty. Dotty could hear her voice, how she'd cry out, "I don't believe it! How on earth did you get here!" Then she'd throw her arms around her friend Dotty and urge her into the house, where they could settle down for a long talk. Dotty reminded herself to introduce Mr. Clarke, and Jud, too, if he behaved himself. Olive would probably want Dotty to stay for at least a week, but she'd have to explain how they got there in the first place and that they had to get back home. She'd show Olive the suitcase, once they'd locked themselves in Olive's room and settled on Olive's four-poster bed.

It would be like old times.

I can hardly wait, Dotty thought, her lips turning up at the corners. I can hardly wait.

CHAPTER 17

THEY FOLLOWED DIRECTIONS AND PRESENTLY SAW A SIGN reading "Boonville: 2 miles." Dotty's face grew warm with pleasure. They were there. Almost. At last.

"Hey there!" A man leaned out of his car. "Get a horse!" he cried.

Jud stood up in the seat, dragging his half of the blanket with him.

"We already did!" he shouted back.

A woman driving a blue Nash honked at them and smiled. Beside her in the passenger seat sat her dog, looking very important, very haughty, like a dowager being taken out to tea. The dog looked them over and, before the car turned the corner, he relented and Dotty could've sworn he smiled at them.

"Oh, I love it here!" Dotty cried. "Everyone's so friendly. I didn't think they would be in such a big city. Olive must be very happy here." She scanned the faces of the passersby in the hope that one of them might turn out to be Olive.

"Where does your friend live?" Mr. Clarke asked.

"Why," said Dotty, astonished, "I don't know. When I write to her, I send the letter to a post office box."

"Well, then, we'll locate the post office and you can run in and ask."

"How about us telephoning home?" Jud said in a hoarse voice. "You promised we would when we got here."

"Right you are," Mr. Clarke said. "You might ask at the post office about where we can find a telephone."

A very clean and shabby old man with tiny periwinkle eyes and dressed in a coat that hung almost to the ground directed them to the post office. Then he ran his hand over Sarah's soft pink nose. "She's a beauty," he said softly. "Used to have one just like her. Got too much for me to feed so I had to sell her." He patted Sarah once more and watched them go, smiling a sad little smile.

"Do you know the Dohertys?" Dotty asked the man behind the post office counter. "They have Box 23. I'm looking for Olive Doherty."

The man stopped sorting letters and gazed at a spot over Dotty's head, trying to think. "Doherty," he said. "What's the first name?"

"Edward. They only moved here a couple of months ago.

108

Six or seven, I think. Olive's my friend. She has red hair and she's about my size. Her hair isn't always red. Only when she's in the sunshine and her mother gives her a vinegar rinse after she washes it." Dotty spread her hands wide in an effort to bring Olive to life. "But at night sometimes it's brown. She wears glasses and she has three older brothers. Her father's a carpenter and he came here because somebody told him there was work for carpenters here."

She ran out of things to tell this man about the Dohertys. He continued to sort letters.

"Good luck is all I can say," he finally said. "More folks out of work here than's in."

What if I can't find her? Dotty thought, for a brief moment panicking. Suppose he doesn't know where to look? What if we came all this way and Olive isn't here? Suppose they moved someplace else if Mr. Doherty couldn't find a job? Oh, my.

She laid her hands on the edge of the counter and stared at the man, willing him to give her the answers she wanted. Just when she thought all was lost, he reached underneath and brought out a piece of paper. "Looks like we got a E. Doherty at number five Carey Street," he mused, running a knobby finger down a list of names and addresses. "Can't say he has a box, but he most likely picks up his mail here. General delivery."

"Oh, please," said Dotty, "how do I get to Carey Street?"

"You alone?" the man asked, looking hard at her.

"No, Mr. Clarke's with me, and Jud. We're only staying the one night. We have to get home because my father doesn't know where I am and he's probably worried."

"Better watch your step over there," the man said. "Rough crowd hangs out around there. You be careful. Don't lose nothing by being careful, my mother used to say."

Dotty shifted from one foot to the other. She didn't have time to waste.

"Could you please give me directions on how to get there?" she said, keeping her voice polite by an effort.

The man shrugged. "Long's you know what you're doing." He went to the door of the post office and, after staring at the sleigh with Mr. Clarke and Jud in it, he said, "Follow this here main street for two blocks. Then bear right, take the next left and you're there. Can't tell you exactly where number five is, but there's bound to be somebody there can. Mind what I say. Watch your step." He turned and went back inside.

"Did you ask him about a telephone?" Jud said.

"I forgot." She jumped up beside him. "We can ask when we get to Olive's. Maybe they have one." She gave Mr. Clarke the directions, leaving out the part about watching her step.

Carey Street was a sad little street. Everything in it was dingy: dingy buildings, dingy snow, dingy sky, dingy people. It looked as if it could use a good wash. The houses leaned against one another like weary people going to sleep with their eyes open. Thin men and women walked dispiritedly along the narrow sidewalks. The sound of Sarah's hooves was loud in the stillness. Dotty felt eyes watching her from behind the murky windowpanes. She saw

110

curtains pulled aside to allow the watchers a better view.

What a place for poor Olive to live, she thought. I wonder where she goes to play. I wonder if they jump rope here, or play marbles or Kick the Can. Or baseball. Or any of the games we played together. I wonder if her friends live here too.

"It's number five," she told Mr. Clarke. Just think. Olive's right near somewhere and she doesn't even know that I'm here too. She doesn't even suspect that I'm getting closer every minute.

"Slow down, Sarah," Mr. Clarke said, pulling in on the reins. Sarah pranced and lifted her feet high. She had a new lease on life. Men passed, their collars turned up, their hats pulled down, their faces and hands red and raw in the cold wind and drifting snow. Some of them stared at Dotty and Jud and Mr. Clarke without interest. Their own misery absorbed all their strength and left no room for anything else.

A group of boys gathered outside a store which advertised "Newspapers, Magazines, and Smokes."

"Can you tell me where number five is?" Mr. Clarke called to them. The boys looked as if he had spoken in a foreign tongue. They turned wordlessly to one another and then looked away. Perhaps they were deaf, Dotty thought.

One boy, bigger, bolder than the others, called out, "Doherty, is it? They're down a ways. On the right. Second floor." He stepped back and was immediately swallowed up in the throng.

Mr. Clarke pulled up his coat collar and once again gave Sarah the go-ahead signal. Dotty felt like getting out of the

111

sleigh and running to find Olive by herself. But she stayed where she was, and after what seemed a year they arrived at 5 Carey Street.

Before they'd even come to a stop, Dotty jumped out, ran up the path, and knocked on the door. She waited, heart doing flip-flops. There was no sound from behind the door. She knocked again. Maybe they were out shopping or something. She knocked a third time.

"Who's there?"

"It's me, Dotty!" Dotty cried, hugging herself. But that wasn't Olive's voice, and it didn't sound like Mrs. Doherty's either.

After another long wait the door creaked open slowly, and an old woman with a face so wrinkled she might've been a hundred years old peered out.

"I've got nothing for you," she said in a high voice. "I give it all away, every last scrap I had. And there's no more food to be had. Except one onion and some celery tops and I'm using those for soup. So be off and don't bother me." She started to close the door.

"I'm looking for Olive Doherty," Dotty said indignantly. "Not for food. They said at the post office she lived here."

The door opened a fraction of an inch. "That'll be the upstairs people then," the old woman said.

"Upstairs?"

"Upstairs is what I said," the woman snapped, "and upstairs is what I meant. Now leave me be." The door closed with an angry bang.

Dotty saw a flight of stairs leading to the second floor of 5

112

Carey Street. "She's up there," she called to Mr. Clarke "I'll run up to make sure she's home and I'll be down in a sec." She leaped up the stairs, feeling this was her last chance. Please be home, Olive, a voice drummed in her head. Please be home. She banged on the door. "It's me!" she cried. "It's Dotty!" As if there were only one Dotty in the world.

"Dotty who?" a voice asked from behind the door.

"Why, Dotty Fickett!" she replied.

The door opened and a woman stood there, her face gaunt and filled with sadness.

"Mrs. Doherty?" Dotty asked. She wasn't sure. But it had to be. Only a few months ago she'd seen Mrs. Doherty, strong and bossy, full of life, wringing her hands as she directed her husband and her sons on how to load her davenport into the truck.

"Mrs. Doherty," Dotty repeated. "It's me, Dotty Fickett."

Mrs. Doherty, for it was she, put out one of her hands. She almost touched Dotty, then seemed to think better of it. Her hand fell to her side and "Where did you come from?" she whispered as if her throat hurt.

"From home. I'll tell you about it. Is Olive here?" If she says no, I'll die. I'll just sit down and die. That's all there is to that.

"Olive?" Mrs. Doherty frowned as if she weren't exactly sure who Olive was.

"Oh, of course. Of course she's here." Mrs. Doherty's face brightened and she looked much younger, more the way Dotty remembered. "Come in. I don't know what's happened to my manners." She stepped aside. "You'll have to forgive me. We don't have much company these days. I've almost forgotten how to behave." She gave a little laugh.

"I know she'll love to see you. She talks about you all the time. All the old days, the good times. Olive!" She raised her voice. "Olive!"

Dotty laid a finger against her lips. "Surprise," she whispered. "I want to surprise her."

"What do you want, Mama?" Dotty heard Olive ask.

Dotty held out her arms, ready to give Olive such a bear hug she'd completely lose her voice for a minute.

"It's me, Olive!" she shouted.

The door opened, Olive peeked out, and when she caught sight of Dotty Fickett, her mouth dropped open, her face bunched together in the middle, and she began to cry as if her heart would break.

CHAPTER 18

OLIVE WAS TEASING. THAT WAS IT. OLIVE WAS ALWAYS joking and kidding around. In a minute she'd stop crying.

Dotty looked at the floor. I shouldn't have come, she thought. It was a mistake. Her stomach felt hollow. She had thought it would be so grand, such a treat when they got together again. She had thought that when she saw Olive after all this time everything would be wonderful. Life would be as it had been before they were separated.

"Don't, Olive," Mrs. Doherty said, her arms rigid and stiff at her sides, as if they'd been starched. "Please don't."

Olive's face was slick with tears as if she'd just come from a very sad movie. She wiped it on her sleeve. "I'm sorry, Mama," she said. Then, "Where did *he* come from?" she asked, her eyes wide with amazement. For a minute she sounded like the old Olive.

Dotty turned. Jud stood there, clutching himself.

"He has to go to the bathroom," she explained.

Mrs. Doherty put out her hand. "I'll show you," she said to Jud.

When they had gone, Olive and Dotty stared at each other. "I can't believe you're here," Olive said at last. "I was going to write you a letter, to tell you—"

"You won't believe how I got here," Dotty interrupted her. "We've got to talk. Let's go to your room and close the door. Like the old days."

But Jud was already back, hitching up his corduroy pants. "How about the telephone?" he said.

"We have to call home," Dotty said, frowning at Jud. "We have to call home to tell them we're all right. Daddy doesn't know where I am."

"My ma will be tearing her hair out in big bunches, she'll be so worried," Jud announced gloomily. He put his finger up his nose in an exploratory fashion, and Dotty knocked his hand down.

"We don't have a phone," Olive said quickly. "Most folks around here don't either. But I think there's one down the street someplace. I'll ask Mama." She flushed. "I'm sorry I can't offer you any refreshments. Mama and I were going to go to the store today. We might have some saltines, though." She opened the cupboard door. Dotty couldn't help noticing it was almost empty.

Boldly Jud said, "How about a cookie?" Dotty stepped on

116

his foot and made a furious face at him.

Olive rattled the box. They could hear crumbs bouncing around inside.

"I guess they're all gone," she said and put the box back. Her hair didn't seem to be as red as it had, and it had lost its beautiful shine. And although she and Dotty had been almost the exact same size, now Olive was at least an inch, maybe more, taller. She was wearing a cotton wash dress that Dotty remembered. Mrs. Doherty must have let down the hem. Even so, it was much too short. Olive's arms seemed to have grown too. The sleeves of her sweater reached just below her elbows and refused to go farther. Her wristbones jutted out angrily, looking for a fight.

Nervously Olive began firing questions at Dotty. "How'd you get here? Why didn't you tell me you were coming? Where'd you get the money for the bus?" As she talked, her face became animated and two bright spots of color appeared high in her cheeks.

"Slow down," Dotty said. "Let's go to your room where we can have some privacy."

"You got to tell Mr. Clarke," Jud said stonily. "He's waiting."

"Who's Mr. Clarke?" Olive asked.

"He brought us here," Dotty said, "in his sleigh. It's very complicated. Go down and tell Mr. Clarke I'll be there in a second. And get the suitcase. It's under the blanket."

Jud thumped out without a word.

"You got a suitcase!" Olive shouted. "Mama! Dotty got her suitcase at last!"

117

She threw her arms around Dotty and kissed her. "Oh, that's wonderful!" she cried. "I'm so happy for you."

Tremendously pleased by this display of affection, Dotty said, "And that's not all. Wait'll you see it. It's beautiful. And wait'll you see what's inside. You'll never believe it, Olive. It's like something in the movies."

"Oh, tell me," Olive begged. "Please. Now. Right this minute."

"Wait till Jud gets back," Dotty said. "Then I'll tell you everything."

She smiled at Olive and Olive smiled back. Coming to Boonville had not been a mistake, after all. It was all right now. Olive was herself again.

Then they heard Jud thudding back up the stairs. He was running.

"He's gone," Jud announced in a flat voice. He looked at Dotty, his face flushed, then his eyes flicked away. "Mr. Clarke's skinned out. Suitcase and all."

"That's not funny!" Dotty cried. She flung open the door and raced down to see for herself.

It was as if she'd dreamed them: Mr. Clarke, Sarah, the sleigh. The street was empty of everything but the dingy snow and an old cat, rummaging through the garbage, its ribs making a pattern underneath its mangy fur. When it saw her, it came to rub against her legs, its eyes full of hunger and dislike.

Dotty raced back. "Why'd you leave it with him?" She shook Jud until his head wobbled back and forth on his neck. Mrs. Doherty came to the kitchen door.

118

"Lands," she said. "Leave him be, Dotty."

Dotty released him, ashamed of herself.

"How'd I know he was a crook?" Jud said. "I thought he was a nice man."

And this time it was Dotty who burst into tears.

CHAPTER 19

A GREAT MANY TEARS WERE SHED THAT DAY AT 5 CAREY Street.

"There, there," Mrs. Doherty said to Dotty. "We'll have a nice cup of soup," and she boiled water, to which she added salt, a couple of carrots, and a cube of beef bouillon.

"We'll let it sit a minute," she said, "to gain strength."

They sat at the kitchen table gazing at one another, speechless.

"How's Mr. Doherty?" Dotty asked, to break the spell. "And the boys?"

To her amazement, Olive put her head down on the table, her arms over her ears, as if they hurt, as if she were trying to drown out the sound of her own sobbing. Her mother got up and went to the stove, looking intently at the soup, willing it to become strong.

"What did I say?" Dotty said, dismayed.

Jud patted Olive on the shoulder, over and over. "There, there," he said to her, in imitation of Mrs. Doherty. "There, there." Jud's voice and patting hand were like a small metronome, marking time.

"I'm sorry," Dotty said. "I didn't mean to upset you. I'm awful sorry." So far, the reunion with Olive could not be called a success.

Olive sat up at last. "It's not your fault," she said, wiping her eyes. "Mama, why don't you lie down and rest? You'll feel better if you do."

"Yes," said Mrs. Doherty. "I think I might." Jud put his hand in hers and escorted her to the bedroom. When she'd gone inside, he gently closed the door and stood looking at it. Olive poured out the soup, and they sat at the table to eat. The carrots floated in the pale brown liquid like little orange Life Savers. Jud scooped his out and when he thought no one was looking, slid them into his pocket.

Olive finished first. She laid down her spoon and said, "My father's dead."

Dotty covered her mouth with her hand. Jud huddled over his soup plate and said nothing.

"Dead?" said Dotty stupidly.

"He had pneumonia. Not very long after we got here. He wouldn't go to bed. He went out every day looking for work. When he couldn't get out of bed one morning we finally called the doctor. But we waited too long. Because we didn't

121

have the money to pay him. That's why we waited." Olive's eyes met Dotty's, then pulled away.

"So he died." She laced her fingers together. "And the boys joined the WPA. You know," she said to Dotty's puzzled look. "The Works Progress Administration that Mr. Roosevelt started, to find jobs for people. They build bridges and dams and Lord knows what all. But they keep busy, and the WPA feeds them, and the work is mostly outdoors so they stay healthy. That's something. We know they're all right, at least. They'll survive. That's what Mama says. They'll survive. And we will too. We all will."

Dotty wanted to reach out and touch Olive, but she was afraid that if she did, Olive would start to cry again. She tried to imagine what it would be like if her father died and her sisters went off some strange place to work and there was no one left but her. And her aunt and uncle too, of course. But the core, the heart of the family would be missing, gone forever. So what if Mr. Clarke had run off with their money? What did that matter now?

"Oh, Olive," Dotty said sadly. It was the only thing she could think of to say.

"Hey, guess what," Jud's high, cracked little voice said. "Guess what I found." He held up a wrapped package. "It's Aunt Martha's hamburger," he said. He sniffed it. "Smells all right to me. Been in my pocket the whole time."

For once in his life Jud turned out to be a blessing.

"Tell you what!" Olive said, jumping up. "We'll cook it. It won't last forever so we better cook it and eat it. Right this minute. We'll have us a proper feast. I haven't had meat in I can't remember when. Is there enough for Mama too?"

"There's plenty. We'll make four nice big hamburger patties and, like you said, we'll have a feast. You got any potatoes? We can boil some potatoes if you have any."

"Potatoes we got," and Olive happily dove down into a paper bag and brought out six potatoes, all growing little horns.

Jud's spoon clanked softly in his soup plate. "Don't forget," he said, holding up his prize, "I brung the meat." For some reason, this sent them off into gales of laughter.

Mrs. Doherty came back into the room. "Sounds like a party," she said wistfully.

"Jud brung the meat," Olive said and that sent them off again. They were making so much noise they didn't hear the knock on the door. Once, twice, three times someone knocked. Then a hand turned the doorknob and the door opened slowly. A man stood there.

"Hey!" Jud saw him first. "He's back."

Mr. Clarke held out the suitcase. "You forgot this," he said. "I thought you might be wondering what happened to it."

"Oh, Mr. Clarke!" Dotty cried, feeling a blush sweep over her face and neck. "We thought you'd gone."

"I went to look for a telephone," he said, taking off his hat. "Had to hunt around but I found one three blocks away in a dry goods store. The proprietor said you could use it long as it didn't cost him anything. Call collect. Tell the operator who you are and the name of the person you want to speak to. As long as that person accepts the charges, you're all right."

"This is my friend Olive Doherty," said Dotty. Mr. Clarke made a small bow and Olive, overwhelmed by his gallantry, giggled.

"And this is Olive's mother." Mr. Clarke took Mrs. Doherty's hand and leaned over it as if he were going to kiss it. Mrs. Doherty looked shocked, then smiled a dazzling smile at him.

"Pleased to meet you," she said. "Will you stay for supper?"

"Thank you, no. I've got to get going. Sarah and I like to sleep in our own beds. I came to say good-bye, Dotty and Jud." He shook their hands solemnly. "It's been a pleasure knowing you. Hope you arrive home safe and sound."

Dotty felt her throat clog. "I'll bring back your suitcase," she promised. "After I get back home, I'll take out the . . . things inside and bring it back to you."

"No," he said. "It's yours. I gave it to you. I have no further use for it. I'm not going anywhere. You keep it."

She reached up to kiss his cheek. "Good-bye and thank you. For everything. You were very good'to us, me and Jud. I won't forget you."

Mr. Clarke smiled and nodded. "Jud," he said, "take care of yourself and of Dotty. Be a good boy."

Jud drew himself up. He shook Mr. Clarke's hand. "Don't worry. I'll see she gets home safe," he said. He drew his brows together and scowled. Dotty looked over at him, smiling. He refused to meet her eye.

"Don't worry," he repeated. "I'll see to it." They all stood there, listening to the sound of Mr. Clarke's footsteps descending the stairs.

CHAPTER
20

MR. EVANS DIDN'T WANT TO ACCEPT THE COLLECT CALL.

"Dotty Fickett!" she heard him holler at the other end of the line. "I don't know nothing about no collect call." She could see his thick red neck and his dirty apron and his outraged expression at such an idea as a collect telephone call.

"Daddy will pay you, Mr. Evans," Dotty said, her voice loud and fast.

The operator's voice cut in. "Will you accept the call, sir?" To Dotty, she said, "I've cut you off, miss. That's the rule until the party accepts the charges."

If you don't, Mr. Evans, I will personally haunt you until

the end of time, Dotty promised silently. I will make you wish you had. You can be sure of that.

Perhaps it was the magic of being called "sir" that made Mr. Evans relent. At any rate, after a lengthy pause, Dotty heard him say in a surly voice, "If her father don't pay up, there'll be trouble. All right, I'll accept the charges."

"It's me, Dotty Fickett," she said in a voice loud enough to carry all the way home by itself. "Please tell my father we're safe. Me and Jud. We'll be home on the bus tomorrow. We're in Boonville visiting Olive, and we're fine."

"Boonville, is it? You got no business going off all that distance without telling your dad. He's been in here, asking if I seen you, and I told him not since yesterday. He was in a state, I can tell you," Mr. Evans said with relish.

Dotty's fingers tightened around the receiver as if it were related to Mr. Evans. "Will you give him the message, please? We'll be home tomorrow," she repeated.

"Slow down. So's I'm sure to get it right. You and Jud are all right. You'll be home tomorrow."

"On the bus. And thank you. You're a good, kind man," she said, making a face at the receiver as she hung up.

"I bet my brother's out looking for me right this minute." Jud's face was doleful. "Bet he's dragging the pond. If it's not frozen," he added as an afterthought.

"That's nice," Dotty said, elaborately sarcastic. "That's a cheery thought for the day. Come on, Olive," and she linked arms with her friend. "Let's go back to your house and talk. We haven't got much time."

They said thank you to the woman who ran the store and walked back to 5 Carey Street. Jud trailed behind, wielding a stick he'd picked up, using it to fight off any wild beasts that attacked him on the way.

"Come on, Jud," Dotty called out. Suddenly it occurred to her that he felt left out. The way she sometimes felt when her sisters ignored her. He ran to catch up to them.

"Here's your nickel, Mrs. Doherty." When they reached 5 Carey Street, Dotty handed back the coin she'd borrowed to make the telephone call. "Thank you."

"You reached your father then?" Mrs. Doherty asked. "He must've been almost out of his mind with worry. I know how I'd feel if Olive disappeared. Especially in this kind of weather." Her eyes seemed to be perpetually moist.

"You've stalled long enough, Dotty," Olive said firmly. "I want to see what's in the suitcase. Now. Not a minute from now. Now."

It was the moment they'd all been waiting for. Tenderly, gently, Dotty lifted the beautiful suitcase from the corner where it had been resting. She sat down slowly and put it in her lap. The others stood watching. Only Jud looked bored.

Dotty snapped open the lid. Under her fingers the clasps were very firm and made of shiny brass. The sweet smell of real leather in her nostrils made her slightly dizzy.

No one made a sound.

"There." Dotty held it out for them to see. The little bundles were all there, packed in the suitcase as neatly and tightly as if they'd been sardines in a can.

"Oh, my." Olive breathed noisily through her mouth.

"Lands," said Mrs. Doherty. "Mercy me." She laid her hand against her heart, as if to quiet it. "I never."

"It's half mine, don't forget," Jud said from where he stood in the middle of the kitchen, legs planted wide apart, hands behind his back, hat still on his head. "It's half mine."

Olive approached the suitcase and laid her hand on the money as if to make sure it was real.

Her mother sat still, her face white, hand still on her breast.

"How much is it?" she said at last.

"I don't know," said Dotty.

"You don't know?"

"I haven't counted it."

"Where'd you get it?" Olive asked suddenly. "Did you steal it?"

"Of course not. What do you take me for?" Dotty said indignantly.

"If I had a chance, I'd steal some money," Olive said.

"Olive Doherty!" Dotty was shocked. "You never would."

"Yes, I would. If I thought I wouldn't get caught, I would. For Mama. Not for myself. Just for Mama so she wouldn't have to always be worried about not having any."

"Don't say that, Olive," her mother protested.

"Why not? Long as it's true. If I thought I could get away with stealing some, I would. If nobody saw me. I wouldn't want to go to jail, though. That's the only thing that'd stop me—going to jail. Otherwise, I'd take as much as I could lay my hands on." Olive looked at them defiantly.

Dotty was shocked. She'd never thought of Olive as

dishonest. Yet now she certainly sounded that way. Back in the old days the question of stealing, of taking something that didn't belong to you, had never arisen. Back in the old days the only problem concerned whether they'd go to the movies on Saturday or Sunday. Whether they'd stay twice around for the double feature. The old days seemed very far away at this minute, very simple in comparison to now.

Nobody said anything. At last Dotty said, "Well, let's count it. Of course, Gary took some."

"Who's Gary?"

"He's this boy who picked us up and gave us a lift in his truck."

"She liked him," Jud said. "She made eyes at him. Then he wrecked up his truck and he was going to rob us and maybe even kill us, so we ran away."

Olive's eyes widened in disbelief. "Shame, Jud. I never knew you told tales."

"It's no tale. It's the truth."

"He's right. Well, maybe he wasn't going to actually kill us"—Dotty spread her hands—"but he sure was going to take all the money."

"Maybe he was hungry," Mrs. Doherty said in a faint voice. "Folks do terrible things when they're hungry."

"He didn't *look* hungry," Dotty said. "Here." She handed around the money. "Everybody count theirs. Then we can add it up."

"Who does it belong to?" Mrs. Doherty asked.

"It might be from the bank robbery in Earlville," Dotty said. "We don't know for sure. But we think it is."

She heard Jud say in a loud voice, "She knows darn well who it belongs to. She knows darn good and well it's the loot from the bank."

"Where'd you hear a word like 'loot'?" Dotty said.

"That's what they called it on the radio."

"Does anyone know you have it?" Olive asked.

"No," said Dotty.

"Then you don't have to give it back." Olive's cheeks were stained dark red with excitement. "You can keep it all."

"I've got an idea!" Dotty cried. "You take half and I'll give back the rest. They'll never know the difference. You need it more'n they do."

Olive looked at her mother. "Please," she said. "Please, Mama?"

Mrs. Doherty stood up. Her back was rigid, her shoulders stiff. She pulled her thin sweater around her. "There's no sense discussing this," she said. Even her voice was stiff. "It doesn't belong to Dotty so how can she give it to us? That's all there is to it."

The room grew very still.

"I'm surprised you didn't hear about the robbery on the radio," Dotty said in a tone of false gaiety, like a nervous hostess who senses the party isn't going well. "It was on a lot. They even interrupted programs to tell the latest details. It was the most exciting thing that ever happened in our neck of the woods. They described what the robbers wore, what they looked like, the getaway car. Everything."

"Did they catch them?"

"I don't think so. Not that I know of. Turn on the radio.

131

Maybe there's something new about the robbery."

"We don't have a radio," Olive said, pressing her bundle of money between her hands as if she were going to make a money sandwich and her hands were the bread.

"You don't!" Dotty was amazed. She and Olive used to spend long hours discussing their favorite programs. Olive had been particularly fond of *Myrt and Marge*, and Dotty never missed Jack Benny or *Major Bowes and His Original Amateur Hour*. After *Little Orphan Annie* and *The Singing Lady*, they were her favorites. Those voices inside the radio belonged to people who were her friends. Why didn't Olive have a radio? Dotty almost asked but thought better of it.

"Anyway, these men robbed the bank, and we saw a big black car like the one they described on the radio, and it whizzed by us and somebody threw something out and it landed in the weeds, and that's when we found the suitcase. Not this one." She patted Mr. Clarke's real leather one. "An old cardboard one that got smashed in Gary's truck."

"I've got all ones," Mrs. Doherty said. "I counted twice and I've got nothing but one-dollar bills. Twenty of them." She laid the money on the kitchen table.

"Nothing but ones!" Dotty said in dismay. Jud's lips were moving as he counted. He was slow in arithmetic. One, two, three, four, five, he counted silently. One, two, three, four, five.

"I've got five dollars four times," he said at last.

"O.K., now multiply five times four," Dotty said unkindly.

He narrowed his eyes at her. "I'm not good at multiplication tables and you know it. And what's more, I bet you weren't either when you were eight." He pointed his finger at her, his face expressionless.

He had her there.

Dreamily Olive's fingers played with the crisp new bills. "I like the way they feel," she said. "And smell. I never smelled new money before. I think I like it better than old." She rubbed the money against her face.

"Once Mr. Clarke was rich," Jud said suddenly. "He told us that. Now he's poor and he says he likes it better." He leaned back in his chair and put his thumb in his mouth and hooked his index finger over his nose.

"Come on, Jud." Mrs. Doherty took him by the hand and led him, unprotestingly, to the couch. "Poor little tyke," she murmured, covering him with a blanket.

"Hey, what happened to your davenport?" Dotty asked, noticing for the first time that the silk-covered davenport wasn't there.

"Oh, that old thing." Olive handed back the money. "Mine's twenty dollars too," she said.

They tallied up the money. There were ten stacks of twenty dollars each. "Two hundred dollars!" Olive said. "Imagine!"

"I thought it might be a thousand," Dotty said. "It would've been if it hadn't been all ones." She felt cheated.

"I'll run out for a little air," Mrs. Doherty said. She put on a sad-looking overcoat that came almost to her ankles, and tied a scarf over her head. She had no gloves, Dotty noticed, or galoshes. "You girls have a good visit while I'm gone."

133

They heard her go down the stairs. After that the only sound was Jud's thumb clicking against the roof of his mouth. Olive and Dotty shuffled the money as if they were getting ready to play cards.

"Let's go into your room," Dotty suggested. "It'll be like old times."

"Why don't we stay here? It's more comfortable," Olive said.

"Oh, please. Let's go to your room. We can pretend we're home, that everything's the same."

"I'd take the money in a minute," Olive whispered, although there was no one to overhear. "But not Mama. You know her. She wouldn't take a peanut if it didn't belong to her." She stared at the wall, her face bleak.

"Come on, Olive," Dotty said, taking her by the hand. "We'll go to your room and have a good talk."

Olive gave her a long, strange look. "All right," she said. "If you want." She opened the door and led Dotty inside. On the floor were two mattresses covered with blankets. There was also a chest of drawers and a small chair. That was all.

"This is where Mama and I sleep," Olive said.

Dotty turned around twice. "Where's your bed?" she asked. "I don't see your bed."

"No," said Olive. Her eyes were very bright, and her cheeks looked as hard and red as two apples. "We sold it. A lady offered us a lot of money for it and the davenport so we sold them both."

Dotty didn't speak. She couldn't. She felt as if it were her bed that had been sold. As if a member of the family had been sold. Things would never be the same again.

In a harsh voice that Dotty had never heard her use before, Olive said, "She offered us seventy-five dollars. It was right after my father got sick. After the boys went away. We needed the money." She shrugged. "It's only a bed," she said in the same harsh voice. Her voice was tight, but her eyes were dry. She looked almost old.

"Tell me about school," she said. "What's Janice Bailey up to? And how about Laura and Mary Beth? They found husbands yet?" She laughed.

And as Dotty began to recount the news from home, Olive's grandmother stared stonily down at them from the wall, her close-set eyes full of disapproval, her thin lips set in a grim smile.

CHAPTER
21

NEXT MORNING THEY ALL GOT TO THE BUS STATION WITH time to spare. Dotty bought two one-way tickets. "That'll be fifty cents," the man said. She handed him a dollar bill.

"She's running late," the man said, handing her change. "Expect the snow's to blame. Can't always get through, you know. Just take a seat. She'll be along."

"Who's she?" Jud said.

The man looked startled. "Why, the bus, sonny," he said as if Jud were half-witted.

Dotty and Olive sat down on a bench that looked as if it might possibly hold them without collapsing. Most of the others had broken slats and peeling paint. An unpleasant odor pervaded the place.

Olive wrinkled her nose. "It smells here," she said.

"Smells?" Jud replied. "It stinks."

There was a door marked "Women" and another marked "Gents." A chewing-gum machine boasted a slot that directed, "Put Penny Here." "If I had a penny, I wouldn't give it to you," Jud muttered, circling the machine, trying to figure out a way to get a piece of gum for nothing.

A shabbily dressed man pushed open the door and shuffled toward the trash basket. He looked over at them, and Dotty was afraid he was going to ask them for money. Apparently, he thought better of it and began to forage through the trash, cursing under his breath.

"You've got to come back," she said to Olive. "You promised. Aunt Martha will find you a place to live. Please say yes, Mrs. Doherty. Please."

Last night Olive's mother had yielded to pressure and said she and Olive would come back to live in Earlville. But this morning she'd changed her mind. Now she pursed her lips and looked at the opposite wall at a picture of a smiling family standing on the running board of a new Chevrolet that could be bought for $445, FOB Detroit.

"It costs a lot to move," she said. "I know Olive's keen on it. And I am too. But they said at the dry goods store they might have a job for me at the end of the month. Their other girl's leaving. It would pay ten dollars a week. I couldn't make that kind of money in Earlville now, could I?"

She knew the answer to that.

I wish she hadn't come with us, Dotty thought. I wish she'd stayed home. She's spoiling our last visit. Why did she say she'd move back to Earlville if she didn't mean it?

"She's coming now!" the man yelled from behind his counter. "I can hear her brakes squealing. She'll be here directly. Better get your bags together. Once she's in, she don't waste time. She likes to get back on the road."

Jud ran outside to get a look at the female bus. He was disappointed to find it was a bus like any other. Dotty picked up her suitcase and, with her arm around Olive, they walked together as closely bound as if they'd been tied with rope.

Mrs. Doherty embraced Dotty and managed to land a kiss on Jud, although he bobbed and weaved rather skillfully in an attempt to escape her.

"We'll think about it," she said.

"Thank you for your hospitality," Dotty said. She looked sideways at Olive because she couldn't bear to meet her look head on. "I'll see you soon," she said. They touched briefly, and then they were hugging each other, crying and laughing at the same time.

"Come on, girls," the bus driver said. "I'm behind schedule as it is. Get on board. We got to go."

Jud climbed the steps of the bus. He stood at the top looking down at them.

"She's running late," he said in a loud voice. "Better get on or she might leave without you." He went to the rear of the bus and took a window seat on the side away from them.

The driver gunned the engine in warning.

"I've got to go," Dotty said and ran up the steps, and the door closed behind her. Leaning over to see out, she waved to Olive and her mother until the bus picked up speed and they disappeared from view.

She walked halfway back to where Jud was sitting. He pressed his face against the murky glass, pretending he didn't know her. They were the only passengers except an old man who was snoring rhythmically and a young woman holding an ugly, fretful baby.

I bet that kid cries the whole way, Dotty thought. I just bet.

She sat down, holding the suitcase on her lap, and put both of her arms around it. The baby started to wail in earnest. But Dotty was tired. She and Olive had shared the same mattress last night, and it had been lumpy and uncomfortable and much too narrow for two people.

She closed her eyes and went to sleep.

CHAPTER
22

DOTTY WOKE AS THE BUS WHIZZED BY ORV BRONK'S
dairy farm. That meant they were almost there. She sat up,
wishing there were some way to get the gritty taste out of her
mouth. She scratched her head and pulled her hat back on to
hide her hair. She must be a sight.

While she'd slept, Jud had been gaining on her. When she
turned, he was in the seat behind her. He scowled and
looked out the window, not wanting anyone to know they
were together. She knew he wanted to be a big shot, wanted
people to think he was traveling on his own.

"Hey, kid," Dotty said, "you got the time?"

Jud pushed his nose against the glass and didn't answer.
She grinned and studied the rest of the passengers. The old

man was gone. In his place were two middle-aged men, their large round faces almost identical. They were dressed differently, but they sat the same way, arms folded over their big stomachs, feet planted firmly in front of themselves, as if they were getting ready to run someplace. They didn't exchange any words, just sat there staring ahead. Dotty wondered what they'd do when they got to where they were going. Tweedledum and Tweedledee, like in *Alice in Wonderland*, she thought.

The ugly baby was quiet, its head lolling against its mother's shoulder.

"Next stop Earlville," the bus driver sang out. Grimly the baby's mother began to fit the child into a sweater that seemed several sizes too small. When she caught Dotty looking at her, a proud look came over her face and she said, "He's going on four months. Big for his age, ain't he?"

Dotty nodded, not having the least idea of how big a baby four months old should be. Thank God it was a boy. With that kisser, it better be.

Her stomach began to churn. They were almost there. She felt strange, as if she had been asleep for twenty years, like Rip Van Winkle, and were coming back to her old home town expecting to find everything and everyone as they had been. Only nothing was the same. Suppose that was the way it was going to turn out? Suppose when the bus pulled into the station and they got off, there was no one there to greet them? Because twenty years had gone by and everyone at home just kept on going. Changing, growing old. Only she and Jud were the same. But they weren't. At least she wasn't.

141

Lots of folks would've moved away. Or died. Lots of deaths happen over twenty years. She didn't want to think about that. Her father would be old. Really old. Maybe Aunt Martha and Uncle Tom would be gone. The girls would be married. Laura most likely to a farmer, with a passel of kids. Mary Beth might've found a rich husband and was living in the city in an apartment with a maid in a white apron and cap to answer the door. Like in the movies. She'd have a fur coat and jewels and two kids, a boy and a girl. They'd be named Buddy and Cissy. Dotty smiled at the thought.

She peered out the window. Everything looked different. The houses seemed smaller, the snow-packed fields much more vast, with little cut-out cows standing in the distance.

"I want to see the money once more." Jud sidled into the seat beside her.

"Your face is dirty." Dotty dove down on him like a seagull after a clam and swabbed his cheek with her grubby handkerchief.

"Owww!" he shrieked.

The bus driver looked at them in his mirror and shouted, "Quiet back there! I don't allow no nonsense on my bus."

The baby's mother, her face grim in the wintery light, joggled the child on her knee. He'd been quiet but began to fuss.

"See what you did!" the child's mother said angrily. "Got him quieted down and you kids start him going again."

"Just leave me be," Jud whistled through his teeth. "You got no right to wash me. You're not my mother."

"Don't you want to look your best when you see your

folks?" To keep herself busy, Dotty breathed on the suitcase and polished it to a fine sheen with her sleeve. It would be the first thing they'd notice. Once they made sure she was in one piece. It was a beauty and no mistake. With a suitcase like that, she could go anywhere. Too bad the initials were R. P. C. instead of D. F. F.

Don't look a gift horse in the mouth, said a loud, strong voice in her head.

Jud's feet drummed nervously. "My ma's going to hit the ceiling," he said.

"Better the ceiling than you."

Jud made a grab for the suitcase. "Let's have a look." He snapped it open before she could stop him.

"Somebody's gone and stole the money!" he cried.

"I gave it to them," said Dotty.

"Who? Who'd you give it to?"

"I left it under Olive's pillow. All except a couple of dollars for us to get home on."

"You had no business!" he wailed. "It wasn't yours! Half was mine. You had no right!"

"They have nothing. Olive's mother'll probably make her give it back. I don't know," Dotty said sadly. "It might help them. They don't have any food or warm clothes or anything. Olive's father died because they had no money for a doctor. We think we're bad off. They don't even have a radio, Jud."

Jud was speechless, overcome.

"We're rich, compared to them."

"We are?"

"Yup. We have enough to eat. Your father has a job. So does mine. We have a car. And a radio. What more do you want? Here." She handed him a dollar bill. "That's half of what I got. It's yours. A souvenir."

He sat staring at the money, turning it over and over in his hand.

"I couldn't have made it without you, Jud." A wave of unaccustomed tenderness toward him washed over Dotty, and she put out her hand to touch him. He jerked out of her reach.

"I know *that*," he said in a voice filled with scorn. "We was partners. You had no business giving away that money without asking. No business at all. Suppose I done that to *you*?"

"I'm sorry, Jud. You're right. I should've asked."

"And I'll tell you something else." Jud stood up and planted his feet wide apart, his hands on his hips. "If you're so big on giving things away, why don't you give the suitcase away? How about that? Just give it away like you give away the money. How about it?"

Dotty gasped. How dare he? It was hers, her heart's desire. "Mr. Clarke gave it to me," she protested.

"Yeah, I know." Jud nodded his head and looked very wise. "But if you're giving stuff away, all I said was why not that too?" He jerked his head at the woman with the baby. "You could give it to her. Bet she could use it. Bet she'd like it for packing the kid's stuff in. Why don't you?" He stood there, watching Dotty, his eyes glittering.

Her arms tightened around the suitcase. She couldn't. She couldn't. It was hers to keep.

Dotty half rose in her seat. The woman was bouncing the fussing baby, her face tight and strained, anxiously looking out the window.

Dotty held up the suitcase.

"You want this?" she whispered, so no one could hear.

The woman kept on bouncing the baby, singing to the child in a mournful monotone. Dotty leaned back in her seat and looked out the window. Her heart was pounding. I tried, she told herself. She could feel Jud's eyes on her.

I tried.

She caught sight of herself in the grimy glass. Who's that sap? she thought. You're some sappy-looking girl, and that's for sure. Nobody's going to take *you* for Shirley Temple.

She bared her teeth at herself in a ghastly smile. Shirley Temple was a movie star. At age six. Lots of folks said she was really a midget and not six at all. Shirley had a head full of golden curls and a face full of dimples. She also was a tap-dancing fool. Folks went wild over Shirley Temple. Dotty wanted to believe the midget story, but in her heart she knew Shirley was really six. Six years younger than herself, two years younger than Jud, and already a movie star.

I will never be pretty. The thought hit her like a small pain under her heart.

I will just be all right. I'll have to settle for that.

I will never use the suitcase. I'll put it under my bed and I'll never use it. Or not at least until Olive comes back and the depression is over and the sadness goes. I'll keep it until Olive smiles again and forgets the bad things and we can go somewhere together. Not to India, maybe, or down the Nile. Maybe to England to find Mary's Secret Garden.

Or maybe just to Utica. Or someplace where they have a skyscraper.

"Earlville!" the bus driver sang out. "End of the line."

Dotty arose and gathered her furs about her. Her train, the Twentieth Century Limited, was arriving from New York City. There were crowds of people, all the home-town folks, gathered to greet her. As the doors glided open and she put one dainty foot on the first step, someone—was it Janice Bailey?—came forward and laid a huge bunch of long-stemmed red roses in her arms.

"Oh, Miss Fickett!" Janice said breathlessly. "I just loved your last movie!" Dotty graciously accepted the flowers. The crowd roared.

Jud inched his way forward. He looks the same, Dotty thought sadly, but he's not. In some ways he's older than I am.

Tweedledum and Tweedledee were the first ones off. The woman with the baby was next. Up close, that kid was even uglier than Dotty had thought. She made a face at him and he drooled back.

She and Jud were the last ones off the bus.

"You won't tell, will you, Jud?" Dotty said. "You won't tell anyone we found the money?"

Jud gave her a long look. Then he leaned down and mashed his nose against the window.

146

"I see them," he said gloomily. "They're all there. Every last one."

"Promise you won't tell, Jud," Dotty said.

"No," he said at last. "No, I won't tell."

Dotty gathered her suitcase to her as if it held great riches, and, her head held high, she marched down the steps to greet her public.

ABOUT THE AUTHOR

Constance C. Greene has been writing for many years, having started out in New York as a reporter for the Associated Press. In 1969 she began to write books for children, and she has since written more than ten books for Viking, including *A Girl Called Al* and *Beat the Turtle Drum*, both ALA Notable Books. She is one of the leading writers of contemporary, humorous fiction for young people. Her most recent book was *Your Old Pal, Al*.

Mrs. Greene and her husband live on Long Island. They have five grown children.